Bad Medicine
By
Roland MacInnis

Book 3
Of the
Quarry Series

Visit your favorite e-book retailer to find other books by Roland MacInnis

Quarry [Book 1]
Bad Man Running [Book 2]
10 Tips for Leaders

Roland MacInnis

Note

Bad Medicine is a work of fiction. Names, characters, places, and incidents either are the product of the author's imagination or are used fictitiously. Any resemblance to actual persons, living or dead, events, or locales is entirely coincidental.

Acknowledgements

My sincere thanks to my wife, Judy, for copy editing, proof reading and for her many helpful suggestions. Thanks also to my adult children, Maura, Margot and Drew who encouraged me throughout. Special thank to friends and family for their continued interest in my writing. Ron McDougall, hmdesign.ca, provided the cover design.

Roland MacInnis

Contents

Bad Medicine

Chapter 1 Gotcha

1907 - Ward 1

Ernie Lundy awoke to a pungent smell and a warm, wet, spray. He jolted upright, ran his hand over his face, sniffed, and yelled, "Piss!"

"Gotcha!" Big Willie said.

Lundy sprang like an enraged bull, and rammed his head into Big Willie's gut.

"Ooofff!"

Willie expelled a gush of wind, jitter-stepped backward, and flopped onto his bed.

Lundy, in long johns, stood over winded Willie. He grabbed an ankle, dragged Willie onto the floor, and delivered a bare footed kick to his ribs. Willie yelped and scrambled under the bed. Lundy kicked, missed, and barked his shin on the bed frame.

"You…you…b…b…bastard," Lundy shouted.

Lundy wiped his face with a bed sheet and a thin scrim of blood, from a ripped incision, smeared his forehead.

Willie cringed beneath the bed. Lundy seized Willie's bare foot in a two-handed grip and Willie slid out. His bare ass showed through the flap of his long johns and he made a desperate last-minute grip on the bed leg.

Lundy braced his feet, leaned backward, and heaved. The bed scraped across the pine floor until it caught in a groove and tipped over. Willie grabbed the bed sheets but Lundy dragged him away. Lundy pounced and Big Willie yelled for help.

A chorus of shouts and screams erupted and Ward 1 inmates scrambled to watch and shout encouragement. The occupants of Ward 1 were the best of the worst of the misfits housed in the Asylum Wing of the Montréal Neurological Institute.

Ward 1 attendants, Hector Lamothe and Joe Yerby, burst from the nearby staff lunchroom "What the hell's going on over there?" Lamothe yelled at the mob.

With Willie's arms pinned, Lundy rained blow after blow into Willie's face, and screamed, "Never again, never again, never again!"

Blood gushed from Willie's nose, and pooled beneath his head.

Attendant Lamothe stood over them. "Get off," he yelled, but Lundy didn't move. Lamothe grabbed Lundy's long johns and yanked hard. Buttons popped and Lundy's underwear peeled half way down his back. Both men tumbled backwards and Lamothe lost his grip.

Bad Medicine

Lundy rebounded, pounced on Big Willie, and delivered several more blows. Each blow sent a fan-spray of blood onto crumpled white sheets.

Lamothe charged and knocked Lundy onto the floor. Lundy sprang and rammed his head into Lamothe's stomach. Winded, Lamothe fell backward, and Lundy poised to take another blow. Attendant Joe Yerby came to Lamothe's aid and walloped Lundy's head with a rock maple club. Lundy collapsed and Yerby helped Lamothe to his knees.

"Get the restraints," Lamothe wheezed through bloody, swollen lips.

Chapter 2 Cadaver

1907 - Medical School

Kathleen Matthews was late for her first class. She hurried down the hall, asked a student for directions, and eventually found the Anatomy Lab. She paused to catch her breath and gave the handle a sharp tug. The door opened with a resounding crack and she stepped into the lab. Heads turned and people stared at her.

Oops!

Snow slid from her boots and melted on the floor. She hurried into the coat room, hung her winter coat, removed her leather boots, and slipped into her shoes.

She took a deep breath, corralled a stray wisp of hair, and walked into the lab. A dozen people ringed a large rectangular table on the opposite side of the room.

What's the horrible smell?

She held a gloved hand over her nose and took short, cautious breaths. She clutched her notebook and walked towards the group. Muddy, wet footprints stained the hardwood floor. There were furtive glances in her direction but she kept her eyes on the man at the head of the table.

Bad Medicine

She squeezed between two young men. One of them reluctantly stepped aside. The other one deliberately squeezed against her and she 'accidentally' found his foot with the heel of her shoe.

Mother was right, I do need sturdy shoes.

"Miss Matthews, I presume," said the distinguished looking man in a black rubber apron.

Dr Antonescu Lupei, her Anatomy Professor, had dark hair, salted with grey but thinning on top. Perhaps by way of compensation for his soon-to-be-bald pate, he had a neatly trimmed goatee.

He peered over his glasses and gestured to his left. Kathleen, feeling embarrassed, moved from her hard won place and stood beside the Professor.

Great! Now everyone can see me.

When she looked around, however, all eyes were fixed on the table. She looked down and, there it was; a dead man, face down, not two feet from her. White drawers covered him from hips to knees and, somewhat incongruously, he wore clean white socks, rolled at the ankles. The back of his head had little or no hair and his face was mashed into a rubber sheet. His skin was mottled with blotches of red, white, and black. He had metal identification tag clamped to his ear and his hands rested close to his body.

Her concentration was broken when Professor Lupei's accented voice said, "Welcome to Anatomy 101."

His 'w' sounded like a 'v' and she guessed an Eastern European origin.

Professor Lupei looked at each student in turn. Perhaps it was her imagination but Kathleen thought he threw an especially long gaze in her direction.

An uncompromising teacher from the old school, he was both respected and feared and did not suffer the ill prepared. The advice from senior medical students was never to miss his class or otherwise attract his attention. Once he knew your name, he had a habit of calling on you for answers in class. Kathleen recalled this advice and regretted her late arrival for this, her very first, anatomy lab.

She saw resentment in the faces of some of the men. The young man, who begrudgingly made room for her, stared at her with his lips curled in contempt.

You may not like it, but I belong here.

Twelve students lined the dissecting table. The only other woman in the class stood on Professor Lupei's right. Kathleen smiled, mouthed 'hello' and received a warm smile in return.

They were the first women admitted to McGill's medical school and it took battles, on many fronts, to gain admittance.

Bad Medicine

Professor Lupei began his lecture by saying, "The best way to learn human anatomy is by dissecting cadavers."

He nodded towards a pleasant-looking, older man who stood opposite him. "Mr. Avila, please begin."

Mike Avila had a dark complexion and short, black, hair, with some grey. He had a fulsome black moustache, flecked with grey.

With a nod to the professor, Avila picked up a scalpel and leaned over the cadaver. Students shuffled aside to give him elbow room.

Kathleen whispered to the young man on her left, "Who is he?"

He whispered out of the corner of his mouth, "He does dissections and prepares cadavers. They call him Cadman."

Avila said, "You'll get to know Ebenezer, inside and out, over the next twelve weeks." There were a few nervous chuckles.

Avila continued, "This lab supports Professor Lupei's anatomy class. You must know anatomy to enable dissection. The purpose of dissection is not exploration, it's to learn anatomy."

Kathleen studied the dead man and thought that his wrinkled skin looked like parchment. He had frizzy patches of white hair on his shoulders and his head was completely bald with a thick bulge at the base of his skull.

He must have been a powerful man in his youth.

Avila continued, "It's important to think before you cut. To avoid mistakes, you must know what's beneath the skin and where body structures lie in relation to one another."

Avila retrieved a scalpel from the pocket of his rubber apron and placed it on the cadaver's back.

Avila said, "I'll make transverse incisions across the shoulders and at the base of the spine. This creates flaps that can be pulled aside."

As he spoke, he ran his right index finger from the base of the man's skull to his buttocks and then traced a path across the shoulders and the top of the buttocks.

Avila picked up the scalpel. "I'll begin the dissection down the midline."

The young man next to her whispered, "Baptism of fire!"

Avila made an incision at the base of the man's skull. Kathleen watched him lay open the midline of the man's back. Then, he made three transverse incisions: across the back of the skull from ear to ear, across the top of the shoulders, and across the lower back. She watched Avila's sure, swift movements and, to her surprise, she didn't feel squeamish. She glanced around the table at her fellow students. Some, like her, were fascinated while others looked away.

Professor Lupei said, "Thank you Mr. Avila. Some of you may find this unsettling, if not repulsive. That's a normal reaction but, in time, you will be as comfortable with dissection as Mr. Avila. Those of you who want to be practicing surgeons will, however, operate on living people. It takes knowledge, courage, and self control to hold a life in your hands and yet do what needs to be done."

The Professor stepped away from the table and said, "That will be all for today."

Kathleen lingered at the dissection table and saw Avila wash the cadaver with a chemical solution that, Kathleen guessed, was the source of the horrible smell. He invited Kathleen to help him slide the body onto a wheeled gurney. He covered it with a rubber sheet and whisked it away.

Kathleen entered the coat room and heard, "Miss Matthews, I'm so pleased to meet you."

Kathleen turned and saw a young woman with short, brown hair, a round face, and an engaging smile.

"My name is Claire Winters," she said, and extended her hand.

Kathleen took her hand and replied, "Please, call me Kathleen. I'm pleased to meet you too."

Claire said, "What did you think of our first anatomy lab?"

Kathleen replied, "I could have done without the cutting on the first day but, I suppose, sooner or later, it had to happen. The men were watching us and probably expected us to faint."

Claire said, "My father owns a butcher shop, so I've seen worse. They think we don't belong, that we're not strong or smart."

Kathleen said. "We'll just have to prove them wrong."

Claire laughed. "That shouldn't be too hard."

Chapter 3 Recollections

Lundy sat on a bed with his head in his hands. He couldn't remember who he was, where he was, or how he got there.

Blood. Something happened, Big Willie, I remember.

He pounded his fist and the smack of flesh against flesh triggered another memory. The man's image, the gold tooth, the sneer, the raised fist.

Mummy! Help me! …Never again, never again.

Her image appeared. She was older, stronger, and towered over him, protecting him. The man smelled of whisky. The images and the memories disappeared but the fear remained. He touched his chest, looking for something.

Where is it…the gold tooth…the ring?

He chased vague recollections of things not right, tantalizing, out of reach. He curled up and covered himself with the dirty-grey blanket. He sought escape, sleep.

Chapter 4 New Guy

Ward 5

"Who's the new guy?" Neil Frost asked.

Roy Egerton swallowed the last bite and chased it down with tea. "He's the mystery man."

"What's his real name?" Frost persisted.

"That's the mystery," Egerton said.

"Don't nobody know who he is?" Davies asked.

"Somebody does, but they're not saying. The inmates on Ward 1 called him Billy Boo Boo," Edgerton said.

Egerton carried his cup and utensils to the sink. "He's definitely crazy."

"Ward 5 crazy?" asked Frost.

"Almost killed an inmate on Ward 1," Egerton replied.

"He seems confused…almost helpless," Frost said.

"Don't let that fool you. If you push the right button, watch out," Egerton said.

"What button?" Frost asked.

"How the hell should I know? I'm not a doctor," Egerton said.

"Just askin'," Frost replied.

Edgerton said, "Orders are, keep him locked up. Take him out once a week and hose him off, bring his food and empty his slop bucket every day."

Frost said, "Why are we so worried about Billy Boo Boo? The Ripper's supposed to be the worst inmate. He gets to exercise an hour a day and gets an occasional shower. Are you tellin' me that Billy gets no privileges?"

"He gets nothing," Egerton said,

"What's his story?" Frost asked.

"They never showed us his file. That's never happened before, it's fishy," Egerton replied.

"Then how in hell are we supposed to manage him?" Davies asked.

"The best we can. Feed him, hose him off, empty his slop bucket, and keep our mouths shut."

"That's it?" Davies said.

"That's it, "Edgerton said.

"Any scuttlebutt?" Frost asked.

Edgerton replied, "They operated on Billy by mistake."

"I thought doctors were smarter than that," Frost said.

Davies interjected, "Some of them aren't as smart as you. Now there's a scary thought."

"Kiss my arse, Davies," Frost said.

Davies looked at Egerton and asked, "Why the big mystery?"

"They're probably afraid of a lawsuit or an inquiry. I've heard the Health Ministry has Dr. Allen on critical review. This isn't the first time he's done something stupid. Dr Allen has been here for two years but, in that time, he's managed to piss everyone off, doctors, attendants, the patients and their relatives. Rumour has it Allen's on a slippery slope. Hiding his latest mistake is just another cover-up. I heard he keeps a bottle in his desk drawer and he's half in the bag most of the day," Egerton explained.

"If I show up fifteen minutes late, they'd fire me," Frost said.

"We need a union," Davies said.

"You got that right," said Edgerton.

Chapter 5 Reporter

Jimmy Moyer savoured the rich leather smell of his new briefcase. It was a gift from Josette, to celebrate his new job as a crime reporter with the Montréal Gazette. The five dollar a week raise meant they would make plans for a family.

Jimmy's editor, Brian Foster, asked him to revisit the Port murders. At dinner that evening, Jimmy said to Josette," This is my chance to make headlines."

Months ago, the vicious murder of two seamen and the stabbing death of a prominent McGill professor gave rise to rumours of a killer on the loose. The killings stopped and the so-called 'spree' was over as quickly as it began.

Weeks passed with no arrests and Foster asked Jimmy to find out why.

"There's a story in this, I can feel it in my bones," Foster said.

It took a call from the Editor-in-Chief to get an interview with Police Chief, Yvan Lévesque. Foster discussed the assignment on the morning of Jimmy's scheduled meeting with Chief Lévesque.

Foster said, "We can't print rumours, get the facts. Why no arrests? What's going on?"

Jimmy left the Gazette office for the interview. He trod carefully on the snow-covered sidewalk and raised his collar, against the cold winter wind. Police headquarters were normally an easy walk from the St. Catherine Street offices of the Montréal Gazette, not so today. It proved a difficult trek because of the freezing temperature and a twenty knot wind. Snow lay in drifts and Jimmy was forced to take awkward girly-hurdle steps to make progress. Instead of arriving ten minutes early, as he planned, Jimmy was ten minutes late. He hurried up the wide stone steps, passed a poorly clad snow sweeper, and opened the heavy door.

He worried about his late arrival, and hurriedly wiped his feet on the doormat. He slipped, and almost fell, when his wet boots hit the polished marble floor. He hustled down the wide corridor and looked left and right for the office of the Chief of Police. Evidence of the recent police department reorganization was reflected in the signs along the corridor: Morality, Murder, Armed Robbery, Major Offences, and Narcotics.

He found the Chief's office and was several steps away when the young woman sitting behind a desk in the outer office noticed him. Her expression slowly changed from quizzical to welcoming. Just inside the door there was a gated barrier with a finely crafted handrail and sculpted balusters.

"Good morning, you must be Mr. Moyer. He's been expecting you," the young woman said and opened the gate.

Jimmy replied, "Sorry I'm late, the weather…" his voice trailed off.

The attractive brown-haired woman said, "I got up early and waded through the drifts so I could be on time but the Chief was still here ahead of me."

She smiled at Jimmy and although her words sounded sympathetic, there was a hint of reproach, maybe a warning, about the Chief's mood.

She nodded towards the closed door, "He's meeting with someone just now, and he shouldn't be long."

She looked at Jimmy with appraising eyes. "I'm Gina, Gina Fellini."

Jimmy replied, "I'm Jimmy Moyer, but I guess you knew that."

She said, "He shouldn't be long, would you like tea or coffee?"

"I'm okay, thanks."

"Please, have a seat," she said.

Jimmy sat near the closed door. Her office was spacious and her desk was positioned close to the Chief's door to make it difficult for anyone to get past her. A black telephone sat on her desk. It was of the newer type with a duck's head transmitter, a dial pad, and a latch-hook receiver. A goose neck lamp sat just behind her typewriter. The decor bespoke a modern 20th century office.

She turned to her typewriter and he guessed her typing speed was well above 100 words a minute.

Judging by the muffled voices coming from the other side of the door, the conversation seemed to be escalating into argument. An authoritative voice yelled, "Just get me the damned information and stop wasting my time."

The door opened and a red faced young man hurried past Gina's desk. She shrugged and looked at Jimmy. She got up and walked into the Chief's office. Jimmy watched smoke coil upward in a shaft of bright winter sunlight.

Jimmy heard her say, "The Gazette reporter is waiting for you."

His reply was unintelligible but Jimmy heard her say, "I know it's past the scheduled time so don't forget your meeting with the mayor."

A voice, presumably the Chief's, said, "Get me the damned file and give me a couple of minutes."

Gina returned, glanced at Jimmy, and retrieved a manila folder. When she passed by Jimmy she whispered, "He'll just be a minute."

Several minutes later, Jimmy heard the Chief yell through the closed door, "Gina, I'm ready, send him in."

She looked at the ceiling, raised her hands in supplication and said, with comic expression, "He never uses the buzzer...Lord give me patience. You can go in now, Mr. Moyer."

The Chief's head was down, buried in a file. He puffed like an idling locomotive.

Jimmy cleared his throat, "Thank you for agreeing to meet with me, Chief Lévesque."

The Chief waved to a chair and mumbled something that sounded like 'have a seat'.

Jimmy sat with notebook and pencil in hand. He looked at the clock over the Chief's shoulder. He felt like an errant schoolboy waiting in the principal's office.

The Chief was a big man with an oval face, deep set eyes, bushy eyebrows and a full head of closely cropped white hair. A thick moustache matched his hair colour. Wide black suspenders hooped over his open-collared white shirt.

Jimmy watched the cigar glow bright red and a puff of smoke obscured the Chief's face. When the smoke cleared, the Chief looked at Jimmy. "Go ahead Mr. Moyer; ask your questions although I think we've already told you people as much as we know."

The Chief looked at the wall clock, "I've got a meeting with the mayor in half an hour so you can have…maybe 20 minutes."

Jimmy opened his mouth to speak but the Chief cut him off. "You're a crime reporter for the Gazette. I've been around a long time and this is the first time we've met. Why is that?"

Jimmy shifted nervously and replied, "I was in sports and I've only recently been assigned to crime."

The Chief said, "You're interested in the Port murders."

Jimmy said, "Yes, there have been no arrests and my editor thinks the public needs to know why."

The Chief said, "There's not much more I can add to what's already been said."

Jimmy said, "We've heard rumours there's a connection between the Port murders and the murder of the McGill professor. Can you comment on that?"

"Rumours, this city is full of rumours. If had to comment on every rumour, I'd do nothing but talk with reporters."

Jimmy checked the clock over the Chief's shoulder, looked at his notebook, and said, "Captain Slocum and Mate Rafferty were murdered within hours of each other, brutally attacked, stabbed to death. That same night, Professor Ducharme, a prominent member of the McGill medical faculty, was also stabbed to death. Might the same person have committed all three murders? Are you any closer to an arrest?"

The Chief frowned. "We haven't been idle. An intensive investigation continues and we think we know who committed those crimes."

"So were talking about one person then?"

"Yes, one person."

"Why haven't you made an arrest?"

"We can't just now, but we're working on it."

Jimmy wrote furiously and asked, "Why not? What's the problem?"

"It's turned out to be a complicated case. We hope to make an arrest soon."

"What makes it complicated?"

"For one thing, there are other jurisdictions involved."

"These crimes were committed in Montréal; do you need permission from another jurisdiction to make an arrest?"

"There are other reasons."

"What other reasons?"

"Our prime suspect is unavailable."

Jimmy frowned and the Chief looked embarrassed.

Jimmy looked down, cleared his throat, and said, "I don't understand. Are you telling me you have a suspect but you haven't been able to locate him or her? By the way, we've been assuming it's a 'him' all along. Can you confirm the gender of your prime suspect?"

"It's a him."

"You said he's unavailable. Does that mean you know where he is but for some reason you can't make an arrest?"

"Something like that."

"What's preventing you from making an arrest?"

"There are procedures to be followed and other jurisdictions to be considered."

"But you do know where he is, don't you?"

"Yes, we know."

Jimmy wrote furiously and said, "So, let me ask again, if you know where he is, why you aren't making an arrest? Aren't you afraid he might escape?"

"He won't be going anywhere."

"What makes you so sure he won't be going anywhere?"

The Chief squirmed in his chair and narrowed his gaze. "Let's just say I'm sure and leave it at that."

"What other jurisdictions are involved? Another country?"

The Chief replied, "Another province."

"What province?"

"I can't say."

"Is he locked up in another jurisdiction?"

The Chief replied, "I can't say."

Jimmy checked his notes and said, "Are you confirming a connection between the port murders and the professor?"

The Chief said, "We're gathering evidence along those lines."

"Are these murders connected, committed by the same man?"

"We think so."

The Chief looked over his shoulder at the clock and reached under his desk. Seconds later, she opened the door and said, "Chief Lévesque, you have an appointment with the mayor and you're already late."

The Chief looked relieved and said, "That's all for now, I have to go."

Jimmy felt disappointed. He couldn't help feeling his lateness contributed to the brevity of the interview. Nevertheless, he had enough for a decent story, at least he hoped so.

Jimmy offered his hand. "I have a few more questions, perhaps we could meet another time."

The Chief gestured to the door. "Check with Gina, she keeps my schedule. Thank you for coming."

On his way out, Jimmy stopped at Gina's desk and asked, "How soon can you get me another meeting with the Chief?"

She offered a knowing smile and said, "I'll have to check with him. I'll let you know."

The snow stopped, the sun was out, and work crews were busy clearing the streets. Jimmy walked back to the Gazette happy with what he hoped would be his first big story. He imagined a headline.

Chapter 6 Headline

Danny Bouvette hurried past Gina's desk. She stood to protest but Bouvette had his hand on the Chief's door handle. Before she could react, Danny entered.

The Chief looked up.

Gina hovered in the doorway, and said, "He ran right by me, Chief."

She struck a pose, received a forgiving nod, and left.

"Have you seen this?" Bouvette asked. He dropped the Gazette on the Chief's desk. The headline read, **Chief Says: 'Can't Arrest Suspect'.**

The Chief looked at Bouvette. "Don't hover Danny, sit down."

With a sigh and a slow shake of his head the Chief picked up the paper. The paper inched upward, like a rising curtain, until it masked the Chief's face. His fingers curled and he crumpled the paper.

"Damn those reporters!" he exclaimed.

With a sweep of his arm, he threw the paper away.

Bouvette said nothing. Long ago, he learned not to fan the flames of the Chief's anger.

The Chief said, "What do you think I should do?"

Bouvette waited. He'd fallen into this trap before.

The Chief's jaw muscles pulsed and, with a huff, he bent down, recovered the strewn pages, and placed the paper on his desk.

"Now what?" the Chief said.

Bouvette paused, and then said, "It's irresponsible of the Gazette to publish this."

The Chief said, "Maybe so Danny, but that's water under the bridge."

"You've been misquoted," Bouvette replied, trying to be helpful.

"It doesn't matter, it's out there, and I'll have to deal with the consequences."

Bouvette said. "Yes, but…"

Gina entered.

She whispered, "George Martin is here."

The Chief grimaced and replied, "Give us a minute, then show him in."

"Should I leave?" Bouvette asked.

"Let's see what he wants. If, as I suspect, it's about the Gazette headline, I want you to be here."

The Chief reached under his desk and pushed the buzzer. Seconds later, Gina led George Martin, Crown Prosecutor, into the Chief's office.

He passed his coat and hat to Gina who, behind his back, raised her eyebrows at the wet footprints on the floor. George Martin tucked his case under his arm and extended his hand.

Pudgy, bald-headed George Martin was the ablest Crown Prosecutor in the Québec Ministry of Justice. He was the Minister's political fixer as well.

They exchanged greetings and the Chief introduced Bouvette. "George, I believe you've met Inspector Bouvette?"

Martin shook Bouvette's hand. "Yes, we've met in the courtroom."

Bouvette replied, "Pleased to meet you again, Mr. Martin."

"Call me George, Danny," Martin replied, with a disarming smile.

George Martin's quiet demeanour masked a legal mind to be respected or, depending on your circumstances, feared.

It puzzled Bouvette that Martin had not attained a more senior position in the Crown Prosecution Service. He had a reputation as a rule breaker and no respecter of position or title.

They sat around the small conference table and the Chief said, "It's your meeting George, what's on your mind?"

George said, "Sorry about the intrusion, Yvan. Thanks for seeing me on short notice. As you might have guessed, it's about today's story in the Gazette."

The Chief said, "The reporter took liberties with what I said."

Martin replied, "No need to explain. I've been there."

He looked around, "We all know how that game is played."

The Chief smiled and visibly relaxed.

Martin continued, "Our political masters, my Minister, and your Mayor, are driven by needs that are different from ours. They need to get elected, they need votes. My Minister spoke with your Mayor earlier this morning, and they agreed something must be done about these murders lest they, and we, are judged incompetent. Nobody votes for the incompetent…unless bamboozled by rhetoric."

The Chief asked, "I assume you have some thoughts on what we need to do?"

Martin opened his portfolio and placed a single sheet of paper on the table. "The suspect mentioned in the story must be arrested and charged. The sooner the better."

"I'm not surprised, "said the Chief.

"Why hasn't an arrest been made?" Martin asked. His tone carried a faint hint of criticism.

Chief Lévesque turned to Bouvette and said, "Danny, please explain the circumstances."

Bouvette wasn't prepared to handle a hot potato but he knew the Chief well enough to know he wasn't simply ducking responsibility. Bouvette looked at Martin and squared up. "The suspect's name is Ernie Lundy. He arrived in Montréal several months ago, using an alias, Bernie Landry. The Sheriff of Cape Breton County, in Nova Scotia, issued a warrant for his arrest for crimes committed there, including murder."

Martin's eyes widened. "You know where he is?"

"Yes, we do. He's a patient at the Montréal Neurological Institute," Bouvette replied.

Martin's eyebrows furrowed. "I don't understand. You'll have to explain."

Bouvette continued, "We need more evidence to ensure a successful prosecution."

"Tell me more, "Martin said.

"Following the murders here, Lundy hid out at the Montréal Neurological Institute. Somebody made a mistake and he underwent a brain operation. He's impaired but it's not clear if it's permanent."

"How did it happen?"

"It seems to be a case of mistaken identity. The Institute is not cooperating," Bouvette said.

Martin leaned forward. "We can solve that problem in a hurry. I'll speak with my Minister and ask him to ask his colleague, The Minister of Health to deal with the Director. I'm sure he'll be more cooperative."

Bouvette laughed. "George, you guys have your ways, I'd appreciate the help."

Martin asked, "Is the suspect behind bars at the Institute?"

"Yes."

"You could arrest him at any time?"

"Yes, but so far we have no direct evidence connecting him to the murders and we can't get a confession until his current mental state improves."

"What about the Nova Scotia crimes?"

"Among other charges, he kidnapped the daughter of TJ Matthews, a prominent Montréal businessman."

Martin interrupted, "I've met TJ Matthews, he's a friend of the Minister."

Bouvette continued, "The warrant alleges more serious crimes, including murder."

Martin said, "Make an arrest. If necessary, use the Nova Scotia warrant."

Bouvette replied, "I'll ask Miss Matthews to identify Lundy as the man who kidnapped her."

Martin asked, "Would she testify in court at trial?"

"I'll ask her when the time is right. She might not want to relive the experience in court. To add to her troubles, Dr. Ducharme was her research supervisor at McGill. His murder came as a big shock to her."

Martin asked, "Does Miss Matthews live in Montréal?"

Bouvette replied, "Yes, she's a student at McGill."

Martin looked at the Chief. "Yvan, here's what you're going to do. Arrest Lundy and I'll arrange a hearing before a judge to determine his fitness. If he's declared unfit, he'll be confined to the Institute indefinitely. If he's fit you'll have to convince Miss Matthews and others to testify. It's important to feed the arrest story to the Gazette reporter."

The Chief nodded.

Bouvette said, "It was a traumatic experience for Miss Matthews. When the time is right…"

Martin frowned and cast and admonishing look at Bouvette. "The time is right because my Minister says it's right, Inspector Bouvette."

The Chief put his hand on Bouvette's arm and said, "We'll do as you suggest, George."

Chapter 7 Identification

Inspector Danny Bouvette approached the receptionist's desk at the Montréal Neurological Institute. A young woman with light-brown hair had her back to him and he tapped on the glass partition to get her attention.

"Good morning," she said, with a half smile.

Bouvette showed his badge. "Good morning, I'm here to see Mickey Clancy."

She said, "Mr. Clancy was here a few minutes ago, he wants you to wait for him in the Chaplain's office."

She gestured. "Down the hall, second door on the right, off the main corridor. I'll tell him you've arrived."

The Chaplain's office had a plain oak desk, a leather covered chair, a waste can and three wooden side chairs. Judging by the dust, it hadn't been cleaned in months.

While he waited, Bouvette examined the contents of the bookcase. He turned when he heard the sound of the door latch.

Kathleen Matthews entered and said. "Inspector Bouvette, so good to see you again."

Bouvette replied, "Thank you for coming on short notice. I hope I'm not taking you away from your studies."

She replied, "I have a class later this morning, I hope this won't take too long."

Kathleen wore a navy-blue skirt, dark blue top and a starched white blouse. Her thin eyebrows and lightly rouged cheeks bespoke careful attention to her appearance.

Mickey Clancy arrived and Kathleen engaged him in conversation.

Kathleen must have sensed Bouvette's eyes upon her because she turned towards him and said, "I'm eager to hear what you have to say, Inspector."

Bouvette retrieved his notebook and said, "We have a suspect for the murder of Dr Ducharme and, with your cooperation, we can make an arrest."

Kathleen looked surprised. "Me, why me?"

Bouvette replied, "I think it's somebody you know."

Kathleen's eyes widened. "I don't understand."

Bouvette said, "You can't repeat what I'm going to tell you."

Kathleen nodded.

Bouvette continued, "There's a man upstairs who Mickey knows as Bernie Landry."

Bouvette looked at Mickey and Mickey nodded.

Bouvette continued, "I believe Bernie Landry is Ernie Lundy, the man who attacked you in Nova Scotia."

Kathleen moved her hand to her mouth. "You mean he's here?"

"Yes, upstairs, locked up," Bouvette replied.

"How did he get here?" Kathleen asked.

"Let's discuss it later. If it's Ernie Lundy, you're one of the few people who can identify him," Bouvette replied.

"Why do you think it's Ernie Lundy?"

"We have circumstantial evidence to suggest that's who he is."

"You want me to identify him?"

"If you identify him, I'll arrest him."

Kathleen looked at Mickey. "You knew about this?"

Mickey nodded and replied, "I knew him as Bernie Landry, he dated my sister, and I never suspected he was someone else."

"How long has he been here?' Kathleen asked.

Mickey replied, "It's a long story, Kathleen. The short story is, somebody made a mistake and he had a brain operation. He may have permanent damage."

Kathleen looked surprised. "Is he still dangerous?"

"It's safe to assume he is," Mickey replied.

Bouvette said, "Would you recognize Ernie Lundy if you saw him?"

Kathleen nodded."Absolutely."

"Will you identify him?"

"Yes," Kathleen replied.

"Now?"

"It's as good a time as any," she said, and reached for her coat.

Mickey stood and Bouvette said, "Mickey has made arrangements. Let's follow him upstairs."

When they passed the fourth landing, Kathleen asked, "Where are we going?"

Bouvette said, "Ward 5, one flight up."

"You said he was locked up," Kathleen said.

"Tight as a drum," Bouvette replied.

Kathleen said, "When I think of what he did to that poor girl in Point Edward…" and her voice trailed off.

Bouvette replied, "I don't want to force this on you, if you have any doubts…"

"Don't worry, I want to do this," Kathleen interjected.

Mickey waited for them outside a door marked **Ward 5.**

Mickey knocked on the door and shouted. "Hector, we're here."

An attendant opened the door and stood aside. Mickey, Kathleen and Bouvette stepped into the ward.

Mickey said to the attendant, "Hector, you met Inspector Bouvette several days ago and now I'd like you to meet Miss Kathleen Matthews. You may have seen her around the Institute; she worked with me on a research program with shell shock victims."

"Welcome to Ward 5, Miss Matthews," Hector replied, and offered his hand.

Hector said to Mickey, "I hope somebody can tell us who this guy is."

Mickey said, "Where is he?"

Hector replied, "At the other end of the ward."

Mickey asked, "The last time I saw him he was on Ward 1. What happened?"

Hector said, "He attacked a fellow inmate, almost killed him. It took all we could do to get him under control."

"Are you ready to do this?" Bouvette asked and moved closer to Kathleen.

She replied, "Yes, if it's him, he must be stopped."

Mickey said to Hector, "Where will we meet him?"

Hector said, "In the lunch room, over there."

Mickey said, "Whenever you're ready, bring Billy to us."

Kathleen gave Mickey a quizzical look. "Billy?"

"Yes, 'Billy'. He was a pitiful character after the operation. Since nobody knew who he was, Billy Boo Boo is the name the attendants pinned on him."

They went to the lunch room and Mickey suggested Kathleen sit opposite the door.

Mickey closed the door and looked through the small window.

He said, "Here they come. He seems calm enough."

Mickey opened the door and Kathleen took a deep breath. She paused and looked as though she didn't recognize the stooped figure walking beside Hector.

Hector nudged Lundy into the doorway and Mickey forced him to stop a few feet from Kathleen.

Mickey stepped aside and Bouvette said. "Do you recognize him?"

Lundy had his chin lowered and Bouvette couldn't see his face. Bouvette gestured and Mickey lifted Lundy's chin.

Lundy had a wild look about him. His hair was long and tangled and he hadn't shaved in several days.

Bouvette watched Kathleen study Lundy's face.

She said to Bouvette. "It's him, it's Ernie Lundy, I'm positive."

She turned towards Lundy and he looked at her with a blank expression. Then, his eyes widened and he lunged at her with his fingers hooked like talons. Kathleen fell into her chair when Lundy advanced. Bouvette slammed his shoulder into Lundy and knocked him to his knees.

Hector exclaimed. "Holy shit! I never expected that!"

Mickey corralled Lundy's flailing legs and Hector said. "I don't know what's gotten into him. He seemed calm enough; I should have used the straps."

"You think so?" Mickey said.

Lundy struggled violently and made unintelligible growls.

Bouvette watched Kathleen cower in the corner and said to her, "Don't worry, we've got him."

Mickey and Hector dragged Lundy from the room.

"He's not going anywhere, you're safe." Bouvette said to Kathleen.

Kathleen nodded but seemed frozen in place.

"Are you all right?" Bouvette asked.

Kathleen took a deep breath. "I'm all right, don't worry about me."

"You're convinced he's Ernie Lundy?"

"It's him."

Mickey said. "Don't worry Kathleen, he's not going anywhere. Ward 5 is the most secure wing in the Institute."

Bouvette said to Mickey, "Thank Hector for me. Tell him I'll be back soon."

"I'll tell him," Mickey replied.

Bouvette continued, "Don't tell anyone what went on here. I'll make an arrest as soon as I get the paperwork."

Bouvette turned to Kathleen. "Might I drive you home or to McGill?"

"McGill, please. I'd be most grateful," she replied.

Chapter 8 Interviews

Jimmy Moyer parted the kitchen curtains and watched early risers shuffle through an overnight snowfall on the street below. In good weather, it was a twenty minute walk to the Montréal Gazette.

"It doesn't look too bad, some snow, not much wind."

"It's cold, so bundle up," Josette replied.

Their cramped two-bedroom apartment sat above Henri Bourassa's tailor shop, at 49 Rue St. Paul. In five years of marriage, they lived in four different places, each one a slight improvement. Josette, a seamstress, worked in the tailor shop and, when the apartment above the shop became available, they moved in. They wanted a family but uncertainties over future income meant a chancy form of birth control, in keeping with the teachings of Québec's Catholic Church. Jimmy's recent promotion to crime reporter, and the five dollar a week raise, improved their circumstances.

Jimmy raised the coffee pot. "Want some?"

"Half cup," said Josette.

Jimmy drained the pot. "I'd better get going. I have a meeting with Brian. He's pushing hard on the murder of the McGill professor and the two murders at the port. He thinks it could be a big story."

Jimmy put on his sealskin coat and mitts and pulled his thick wool tuque over his ears. He took pride in his 'coureur du bois', winter-ready, appearance.

Josette sat at the table in her flannel nightgown. Jimmy bent low and kissed her.

"I love you," he said. He gently touched her cheek. "Until tonight."

★★★

The Gazette

Jimmy looked through the grimy interior window of the newsroom, hoping to find City Editor Brian Foster. Foster was hard to track down at the best of times. He buzzed around, as Jimmy's mother used to say, 'like a blue-arsed fly'. He dogged reporters, discussed stories, proofread columns, and chased leads. Jimmy didn't see him in the newsroom, and he walked the length of the hall to Foster's office.

Foster's door was closed, and the shade was down. Jimmy stood outside the door and listened to the rumble of voices. He put his hat and mitts in his coat pocket, leaned against the wall, and waited. Ten minutes later the door opened and Pudgy, a Gazette photographer, backed into the hall. Foster's voice followed Pudgy. "No more excuses! Get the damned picture! If he's fooling around with his secretary, I don't care who he is, I need a picture."

Pudgy saw Jimmy, and averted his eyes. He bounded away with an embarrassed glance over his shoulder.

Jimmy stuck his head in the door, "You free now?"

Foster scowled and took a deep breath. "You might as well come all the way in, take a seat, give me a minute."

Jimmy draped his coat over the chair and sat down.

Foster's office was a mess: his bookcase held everything but books. Old newspapers covered every table, desk and chair. The place hadn't been cleaned or dusted in months, perhaps years. An out-of-date photograph of Foster's wife sat on the windowsill, her shy smile refracted in cracked glass. Beyond the cobweb-covered window, the windowless brick wall of the printing plant choked off any available light.

Foster was bent over a mock-up of the city section of tomorrow's newspaper. He ran an ink-stained finger up, down, and across. He mumbled, squawked and occasionally slashed, with a thick blue pencil.

Foster said, "Your story is hot and you gotta strike while it's hot. Did you make that connection?"

"You mean connect the dead professor?" Jimmy said.

"Exactly, we talked about this. Have you got anything new?" Foster asked.

Jimmy felt uneasy. He regretted waiting for direction without doing much of anything. Under the barrage of Foster's questions, he acknowledged lost momentum on the story. It was, he thought, a mistake he would remember.

He stammered, "Well… I thought… maybe… I'll talk to Chief Lévesque again… you know… follow up."

Foster scowled. "Get on with it Jimmy. Talk to the police. Have any arrests been made? Go to the port. What was going on there? Get background on the two murdered guys. Any drugs? Gang involvement? Dig, Jimmy… dig, that's what reporters do. Don't stop until you have a great story…dig…dig!"

Jimmy fumbled inside his case. "I'll get right on it," he said.

Foster looked at his watch and let out a deep sigh. "Move, Jimmy, move! Get on with it! I want something juicy."

Bad Medicine

Before Jimmy could rise from his chair, Foster said, "I'm late for a meeting. You're doing a good job, Jimmy. Remember, one good interview leads to another, follow the leads. Go where the story takes you. Dig!"

Jimmy crammed his notebook into his case and bolted out the door. He went to the newsroom, grabbed a telephone, and called Chief Lévesque's office.

He recognized Gina Fellini's voice. "Hello Gina, it's Jimmy Moyer from the Gazette. I'd like to meet the Chief again."

"The Chief is busy and won't be able to meet with you."

Jimmy laughed, "When, then?"

"The Chief is a busy man…"

Too busy, my ass.

Gina continued,"…he's asked Inspector Bouvette to deal with it."

"Could you put me through?"

"Call the switchboard."

She's not making this easy.

"Do you have the number?" he asked.

"It's in the book."

Jimmy felt a sudden urge to slam the switch-hook in her ear

"Thanks, Gina," he said, through clenched teeth.

He called Bouvette's number several times over the next hour. Each time he called, someone promised to deliver a message. He couldn't get anyone to tell him where the inspector was or when he was expected back. In between calls, he sat at his desk and developed questions.

Finally, just after noon, Bouvette answered and agreed to meet the next morning.

***

Montreal Police Station

Jimmy arrived at the station at 8:45 AM and was escorted to an interrogation room. Its furniture was sparse, a plain table with a chair on either side and another chair near the door. A naked bulb hung above the table. Jimmy placed his notebook on the table and waited. At 9:15 AM, feeling impatient, he left the room and found the desk sergeant.

"He's in his office, he'll be with you soon," the sergeant said.

Jimmy returned to the interrogation room and was surprised to see Inspector Bouvette waiting for him.

Jimmy stammered, "I… was just… looking for you."

"I was busy, let's get started, I have a staff meeting in about thirty minutes," Bouvette replied.

Jimmy put his hand on the back of a chair and Bouvette said, "I've been sitting on my ass all morning, do you mind if we have this conversation standing up?"

"No… not at all," Jimmy said.

Bouvette said. "I understand you want to talk about the murders."

"Have there been any new developments since I met with Chief Lévesque?" Jimmy asked.

Bouvette flashed a knowing grin. "Yes, we've laid charges and made an arrest."

"Who was arrested?"

"A man called Ernie Lundy."

"What charges?"

"Crimes committed in Nova Scotia."

"Not here? Not the Port and or Prof. Ducharme?"

"No."

"Is Lundy a suspect?"

"Off the record?" asked Bouvette.

"Yes, agreed."

"He's our main suspect."

"Why do you suspect him?"

"Evidence."

"What evidence?"

"Can't say."

"What was his connection to Professor Ducharme?"

"We haven't established that."

"Tell me about Ernie Lundy," Jimmy asked.

"Lundy arrived in Montréal several months ago and used an alias to get a job at the port. He joined the West End Gang. Prior to his arrival in Montréal, he was employed as a quarry manager in Nova Scotia. He committed several serious crimes there and we have arrested him on the basis of their warrant."

"You said you had more work to do in relation to these murders in Montréal. What work?"

"To gather evidence."

"Do you have a confession?"

"No, he hasn't confessed."

"Have you questioned him?"

"Not really, it's complicated."

"He's a suspect. He's under arrest. What's the problem?"

"There are…."

Bouvette looked up at the ceiling. "certain… medical issues."

"He's too ill to be questioned?"

"In a way, yes."

Jimmy pulled out a chair and sat down. He looked at his notes. He sensed Bouvette's evasiveness.

What's he hiding?

Jimmy asked, "Why don't you just come clean and tell me what's going on?"

"I assume we're still off the record," said Bouvette.

Jimmy replied, "If you mean I can't publish exactly what you say and attribute it to you, the answer is, yes. However, I will use your information to support my story and guide my interviews with others."

"Very well, here it is. He's being held at the Montréal Neurological Institute pending a hearing to determine fitness to stand trial."

"He's insane?"

"I'm not a doctor. It's not my job to make that determination."

Jimmy made a few notes and said, "Do you have witnesses?"

"Off the record?"

"Yes."

"We haven't found any. The evidence is largely circumstantial."

"What about his Nova Scotia crimes?"

"They are numerous, very serious, with witnesses and evidence."

Jimmy turned a page in his notebook. "What witnesses?"

Bouvette looked uncomfortable. "A witness, one of his Nova Scotia victims."

"Can you name the witness?"

"No, I can't."

"Why not, we're off the record."

"I can't do it, not even off the record."

"Why not?"

Bouvette held up his hand. "Please, just leave it at that."

Bouvette looked at his watch. "I have to go."

Jimmy said, "Thank you, Inspector. I may need to interview you again."

"Contact Gina, she'll make arrangements."

They shook hands and Bouvette left the room.

★★★

Port of Montréal

An hour later, Jimmy Moyer sat in the office of Ian English, Head of Security at the Port. A burly ex-policeman, with a square chin, English's blue shirt bulged around his biceps. His thinning hair was chopped short and his eyes were piercing and intelligent. English had a chipped front tooth, and Jimmy surmised that this man had met his share of tough guys.

Jimmy began. "As I said, it's about the murders of the two seamen."

English's response was a half-hearted shrug.

Jimmy waited several seconds for a reply and, receiving none, he said, "I met with Inspector Bouvette about these murders."

English smiled politely but said nothing.

Jimmy reflected on English's non-response and guessed if you asked no questions he gave no answers.

Jimmy asked, "What has been your role in the investigation?"

English answered, "A limited one. When the bodies were discovered, the Montréal police took over the investigation"

"Who discovered the bodies?"

"The body of Capt. Slocum was discovered by the ship's watch."

"I was led to believe two members of the ship's crew were murdered that night."

"Mate Rafferty was murdered in the city, not at the Port."

Jimmy looked at his notebook. "Do you have any idea what motivated these murders?"

English grinned. "None whatsoever."

Jimmy asked. "Were drugs involved?"

"I don't know. I doubt it."

Jimmy said, "The police have arrested a suspect. Can you confirm someone by the name of Bernie Landry worked here?"

English frowned. "I don't have the information at my fingertips. Perhaps I can get it to you later."

Jimmy nodded. "What can you tell me about West End Gang activity at the Port?"

English leaned forward. "We're aware that certain criminal elements, the West End Gang among them, have targeted the Port, and we've taken additional security measures.

"I'll take that as confirmation the West End Gang has a presence here."

"Suit yourself," English said, with an expression of feigned interest.

Jimmy looked over his notes and said, "I've got a deadline to meet. I may want to meet with you again to clarify some of the details."

English nodded, "Good luck with your story."

★★★

The Gazette

Later that afternoon, Jimmy met with Foster and reviewed progress.

"What's new?" Foster asked.

Jimmy summarized his interviews with Inspector Bouvette and Ian English.

Foster pulled up a chair. "I can persuade the editorial committee to give us the front page on this. You'll have to hang your story on Lundy's connection to the Montréal murders, especially the Professor. Make it clear there will be surprises to come."

Jimmy felt a jolt of adrenaline. "I'll write it up for you."

A front-page story! I'm onto something.

Foster said, "Get in touch with someone at the Halifax Chronicle. Find out what happened in Nova Scotia. They must have published something. Find out what they know. If necessary, trade what you know for what they know."

Foster's face expressed a friendly warning. "Don't let them scoop you."

"I'll send a telegram right away."

"We can't wait, use the telephone, long-distance."

"Long-distance, it'll be expensive."

"It's a big story, just do it."

***

The Chronicle

"Halifax Chronicle, good afternoon," said the voice on the other end of a poor connection.

Jimmy raised his voice. "I'm Jimmy Moyer, a reporter with the Montréal Gazette, I need to speak with your editor, it's important."

Jimmy heard the intermittent buzz and clatter of the newsroom in the background while he waited for the editor.

"Harold Fleming," said a gruff voice on the other end of a crackling connection.

"Thanks for taking my call, Mr. Fleming. I'm with the Montréal Gazette."

"Moyer?"

"Yes, Jimmy Moyer. How's the connection?"

"A bit noisy, but I can hear you well enough."

"I'm working on a story about three brutal murders in Montréal and there's a Nova Scotia angle I'd like to ask you about."

"Go ahead, what's the Nova Scotia angle?"

"A man named Ernie Lundy has been arrested here on a warrant issued by a Nova Scotia sheriff. Lundy was a quarry manager in Cape Breton and, somehow, escaped arrest. Have you published anything?"

"Indeed we have, it was a big story," Fleming replied.

"I'm looking for more information about Lundy's activities in Nova Scotia."

"Before I say anything further, would you agree to share your information with me," Fleming asked.

"Yes, I will. I'm still working on it and I'll share it with you on the condition you not publish anything before we do."

"Agreed. Send me a telegram the day your story is published."

"Agreed. Now, tell me about Lundy's Nova Scotia crimes."

"Ernie Lundy worked for TJ Matthews, who owns a limestone quarry in Cape Breton. Matthews is a big shareholder in Dominion Steel. Matthews' daughter was kidnapped, assaulted, and subsequently rescued. As you probably know, TJ Matthews is a prominent Montréal businessman. In order to get the story we had to agree not to publish the names of anyone in the Matthews family."

Jimmy felt a surge of excitement. "Where is Matthews' daughter now?"

"I'll check our files, but I believe she is or was a student at McGill."

Jimmy wrote furiously, then asked, "What's her name?"

"I don't remember. I'll look it up and send you a telegram."

"Could you do it right away? I'd like to file a story this week."

"I'll do it. Be sure to let me know when your story is published?"

"Yes, I will. Thanks for your help. We'll talk again, I'm sure."

Chapter 9 Incident

Professor Lupei's original seating plan placed Kathleen and Claire on opposite sides of the classroom where they were subjected to practical jokes and nasty comments. Malcolm Paul was a ringleader and he took particular pleasure in their discomfort. He wasn't alone in his prejudice since the medical school was divided on the issue of women in medicine.

Several embarrassing incidents prompted them to approach Professor Lupei for a new seating arrangement.

"Why do you want to sit together?" the professor asked, pronouncing 'want' as 'vant'.

Kathleen decided not to reveal the true reason for the requested change, since she wasn't yet sure which side of the controversy Professor Lupei supported. Instead, she said, "We've decided to study together and it will help us with note taking."

The professor agreed and their seating was changed. The two men who gave up their seats did so reluctantly. Amidst the seat shuffling, Malcolm Paul couldn't resist a parting shot, "Even if you sit together, you'll still only be as smart as one man."

On the first day of their new seating arrangement, Kathleen held the door until Claire caught up and, together, they entered Professor Lupei's classroom. They took their seats before Professor Lupei's appearance, and cast wary eyes towards Malcolm Paul and his cohorts. Kathleen saw Claire squirm and reach beneath her bum. Claire cautiously withdrew her hand, as if afraid of what it held. Kathleen caught a whiff of formaldehyde and curled her lips in disgust when she saw the wrinkled, fleshy object in Claire's hand. Claire emitted a yelp and threw a shrivelled cadaver penis over the heads of the students seated in front of her. It landed on the floor with a splat, just as Professor Lupei entered through a side door near the lectern.

Professor Lupei stopped, looked down and then and looked at Claire. He reached into his lab coat, retrieved a rubber glove, and picked up the offending object. Suppressed laughter came from Malcolm Paul and his friends.

The professor held the ugly looking object between his thumb and forefinger and frowned at Claire Winters who hid her face in her hands. Lupei walked to the lectern, picked up the seating plan and ran his finger down the page.

He looked at Claire and said, "Miss Winters, this classroom is devoted to the serious study of human physiology. Please leave the room."

Claire protested her innocence but Professor Lupei, unmoved, responded with a dismissive gesture. Kathleen touched Claire's arm and said, "Don't worry."

Claire picked up her books and, with head down, squeezed past seated students and left. Kathleen watched Claire's departure, and caught a glimpse of a smirking Malcolm Paul. Kathleen fixed her gaze on him until their eyes met. She narrowed her eyes and mouthed the worst epithet she could think of.

Afterward, Kathleen saw Claire seated on the window ledge opposite the classroom. She sat beside her and moments later, Malcolm Paul and his friends appeared.

Claire said, "Let's go, Kathleen, I don't want to give them the satisfaction of seeing how upset I am."

Kathleen replied, "I think he's determined to make us quit. He doesn't know me very well, because it's the last thing I'd do."

Claire said, "Nor would I. His father is on the Board of Governors and he acts as though he's got special privileges."

Kathleen replied, "My father is also on the Board but I certainly don't feel it gives _me_ any privileges. People should succeed in life on their merits."

"Let's go, I can't stand being around these people," Claire said.

 ★ ★ ★

Chapter 10 Shell Shock

Kathleen read Professor Merrick's note and felt hopeful. He promised her a Research Assistant position contingent on approval of funding for his research proposal. Following the controversy over Professor Ducharme's approach and his subsequent murder, the Canadian Army asked the Medical School for an alternative approach to the treatment of shell shock. Professor Merrick proposed a psychiatric approach and Kathleen hoped she would have an opportunity to work with him.

She waited outside Professor Merrick's office door and watched students and faculty bustle up-and-down the busy corridor. Claire Winters emerged from Professor Lupei's office and Kathleen called out to her.

"How was it?" Kathleen asked.

Claire replied, "I was as nervous as a kitten when I walked into his office. However, to my surprise, he was quite understanding. He knew the men in the class made life difficult for us."

"If he understood, why did he kick you out of class?"

"He said classroom discipline was vital to the teaching process and he had no choice, given the circumstances. He found out later who started the incident and, although I might have handled it better, he understood."

"Is everything okay now?"

"Yes, I think so," Claire replied.

Looking over Claire's shoulder, Kathleen saw Professor Merrick emerge from Dean Harcourt's office.

"Here comes Professor Merrick, I have a meeting with him," Kathleen said.

Claire said. "I'll see you later."

Dr Sean Merrick, a highly regarded teacher and researcher, believed in a psychiatric approach to the treatment of mental illness. He disagreed with Doctor Ducharme's use of opiates for shell shock. During his postgraduate work in neurology at McGill, he read Sigmund Freud's, books and he believed that Freud's insights into the workings of the human mind signalled a new era in the treatment of mental illness.

Kathleen and Professor Merrick shared a small conference table in his office.

He said, "I have some good news for you Miss Matthews. My proposal to treat shell shock victims will be funded by the Canadian Army."

She said, "I'm very pleased to hear it. Congratulations!"

"I'm assuming you will accept the Research Assistant position."

Kathleen was barely able to contain her excitement. "Yes, I'd like it very much,"

He passed a document to her. "This document outlines the program. I'd like you to help me with clinical trials. Your experience with shell shock patients means we will be able to begin without undue delay."

"When does the program begin?" Kathleen asked.

"I'm hoping to begin in a week or so, depending upon the cooperation of the Institute in making trial patients available."

"I can't wait," Kathleen said.

"Could we meet next Monday morning?"

"I have a class from 9 AM to 10:30 AM," Kathleen said.

"What about 10:45 AM?"

"I'll see you then," Kathleen replied.

Chapter 11 Story

Jimmy Moyer hovered in the doorway.

Brian Foster said, "Come in, Jimmy, I was expecting to see you yesterday."

"I've been busy with the story," Jimmy replied.

"You talked with the Halifax Chronicle?"

"Yes, I got some good information."

"What did they tell you?"

"Lundy, worked for TJ Matthews and he kidnapped and assaulted his daughter."

"What happened to her?"

"She recovered and returned to Montréal. She's a medical student at McGill."

"See if you can get her side of the story."

"Is there a particular angle?"

"She's the daughter of a prominent businessman and that, in itself, is of interest. Get as much information as you can about what happened. There must be something to tie Lundy to the Ducharme murder. Find out what it is."

"What about TJ Matthews?"

"I believe he's a friend of our publisher. I don't think it's a problem but I'll find out."

"How's the story playing upstairs? Getting any traction?"

Foster's face lit up. "It's a great story. The editor loves it. He thinks it has legs and will play for weeks, if we handle it right. You'll have to work hard, find new angles, and keep it fresh."

"I'll work the drug angle, the West End Gang, Lundy's work at the port," Jimmy suggested.

"Good idea, if the West End Gang is involved, I have a confidential source that might help you. Let me know and I'll put you in touch."

"I'll start with Matthews' daughter and see where it leads."

Chapter 12 Questions

Medical Building

Jimmy Moyer wiped his snow-covered boots on the mat and walked down the corridor.

Two young men sat on chairs outside an office.

Jimmy approached them and said, "Excuse me, I'm looking for Kathleen Matthews."

"Is she a student?" one of them asked.

"Yes, how can I find her?"

He pointed down the corridor. "Go to the Dean's office, the secretary has a list of students."

"Thanks," Jimmy said.

A few minutes with the receptionist resulted in Kathleen's class schedule and directions to her classroom.

Moments later, Jimmy stood outside room M-13. He cracked open the door, the class was in session and he peeked in. A dozen students watched a professor write on the blackboard. There were two women in the class and one of them had to be Kathleen Matthews. He crossed the corridor, sat on the window ledge, and waited for her.

A crescendo of voices signalled the end of class. The door opened and a swarm of students emerged. Two young women were last out. It was lunchtime and they walked quickly so Jimmy hurried to catch up. He heard one of them say to the other, "I'm meeting a friend."

The other one replied, "Goodbye Claire, see you later."

When the two women separated, Jimmy approached and asked, "Excuse me, are you Kathleen Matthews?"

Her eyes puzzled over his face. "Who wants to know?"

"My name is Jimmy Moyer, I'm a reporter for the Montréal Gazette."

Kathleen frowned and tilted her head. "What do you want, Mr Moyer?"

"I'd like to ask you a few questions. Perhaps we could find a quiet place to talk."

"Questions about what?"

Jimmy sensed her wariness.

"About being one of the first woman admitted to medicine at McGill."

She smiled and looked relieved. "I can't believe my story would be of much interest to anyone."

"Of course it would… human interest…women's progress…"

She looked around. "I don't have much time. I haven't had anything to eat, and I have a lab in less than an hour," she said.

"It won't take long, we can talk over lunch," Jimmy suggested.

"The student cafeteria isn't very private," she replied.

He sensed her reluctance and persisted. "What about a café close to the campus?"

She bit the corner of her lip and looked skeptical.

Jimmy pleaded. "I'll buy, it shouldn't take long, just a few questions, please."

"I know a place, it's close, but I'll have to be back before 2:00 PM," she said.

They sat in a far corner of Le Coin, a small café close to the McGill campus. Kathleen ordered a sliced chicken sandwich and a glass of milk. Jimmy ordered a bowl of pea soup, with coffee to come later.

Jimmy reached into his pocket and counted his money. He had just enough to cover the meal with a bit to spare. He hoped Brian Foster would reimburse him.

While they waited, he placed his notebook on the table and pressed a clean page. "How does it feel to be among the first women in medicine?"

She replied, "It's hard to describe how I feel. Even as a little girl, I dreamed about being a doctor."

Jimmy asked several more questions related to her experience at McGill.

She fidgeted and looked over her shoulder. "I hope the food comes soon, I don't want to be late for my lab."

Jimmy caught the attention of the waitress, then turned back to Kathleen. "Getting admitted was quite an achievement, it couldn't have been easy."

"It wasn't but, fortunately, I received a great deal of support along the way."

The waitress delivered their food and they began to eat. For a minute or two they ate in silence, then Jimmy decided to take their conversation in a different direction. "Did you get much encouragement from your professors?"

"Yes, from some."

"Which ones in particular?"

She looked thoughtful, took a bite of her sandwich and chewed slowly.

He asked, "Some of your professors encouraged you, which ones?"

She swallowed. "Professor Harcourt was very helpful."

Her response was slow and somewhat evasive.

"Was Professor Ducharme helpful?"

Her expression quickly changed. She stared at Jimmy and chewed even more slowly.

Jimmy waited.

She took a drink of milk.

Finally, she said, "Yes, Professor Ducharme encouraged me, but it was Dean Harcourt who opened the door."

Jimmy said, "Professor Ducharme's murder remains unsolved. The Montréal Police haven't made any arrests."

She took another bite, chewed and swallowed. "I don't know anything about it."

"I understand Professor Ducharme did research on opiates?"

"Yes, he wanted to relieve the suffering of the mentally ill."

"Did you work with him on opiates research?"

"Yes, I was a graduate student and he was my research supervisor."

She shifted uncomfortably and reached for her coat. "I'm late, I've got to go."

She stood and Jimmy said, "A man by the name of Ernie Lundy is a patient at the Montréal Neurological Institute. He's been charged with crimes committed in Nova Scotia."

Jimmy expected a strong reaction but she didn't flinch.

"I hope I didn't upset you, Miss Matthews. Let me explain."

"There's nothing to explain," she said. She jammed her arms into the sleeves of her coat and hurried out the door.

Jimmy threw some money on the table and chased after her. He caught up as they approached the wrought iron gates at the entrance to the McGill campus.

"Miss Matthews, please, let me explain," he shouted.

He walked past her, turned around, and walked backwards. "At some point, I'm going to write about Ernie Lundy. The police are gathering evidence and, I expect, they may charge him with Dr Ducharme's murder."

She brushed past him. "That has nothing to do with me!"

Jimmy caught up with her. "Perhaps not, but the story of his crimes in Nova Scotia has been published by the Halifax Chronicle. Your name wasn't mentioned, but I've been told you were one of his victims."

Her calm exterior eroded. "Yes, I was a victim. I'm still a victim. If you write about me, I'll be a victim for the rest of my life. Leave me alone! Go away!"

Jimmy felt a twinge of conscience but needed information for his story.

He said, "The murder of Professor Ducharme is a matter of public interest and, sooner or later, someone will write about it. Tell me what you know about Lundy and I promise my story won't embarrass you or your family."

She shook her head, "I can't do it. I have a class, I've got to go."

She walked away.

Jimmy pursued her. "If you tell me about Ernie Lundy, I'll keep your name out of my story."

"I don't want to talk about it."

"I need some background on Lundy. I'm writing a story about the murders in Montréal. If he's as bad as they say, he'll face justice and the public needs to know. Tell me about Lundy, what did he do in Nova Scotia?"

She said, "I can't do that!"

"One way or another, the story is going to be told. If it isn't me, it'll be a reporter from another paper. You can go off the record and you or your family will not be mentioned."

She said, "How can I believe you?"

"My editor will put it in writing, if it would convince you."

"I want time to think about it."

"Okay, take some time. However, it won't wait forever. Do you have a telephone number where I can reach you?"

Jimmy wrote her telephone number in his notebook.

Chapter 13 Restrained

Lundy woke and immediately recalled snippets of his confrontation with the skinny attendant. These moments of clarity happened more often and, when they did, he felt better.

He stood on his tip toes and hooked his fingertips over the edge of the window sill. He pulled himself up and caught the promise of sunrise. His arms tired and he lowered himself to the stone cold floor.

He shuffled to the door, pushed the food slot, and pressed his ear to the opening. A rumble of voices came from the attendant's lunchroom. He sat on his metal frame bed with his back to the wall and his knees tucked under his chin.

The clatter of utensils and the clacking, bockety wheel of the meal cart announced breakfast. He crept to the door and listened for the rattle of keys.

"Back!" shouted the skinny one from the other side of the door.

Lundy crouched down and watched the door slot open.

The food tray poked through and the skinny one shouted, "Take it!"

He saw the skinny one and, behind him, the bushy-bearded fat one.

Lundy grabbed the tray, and sat on the floor. He picked up the bowl of mush and greedily shovelled handfuls into his mouth. It was lumpy and smelled like rotted fish, but there was plenty of it and it satisfied his hunger. He gnawed the dried crust of bread and finished off the cold tea. He left the metal tray and dirty tin dishes on the floor. The springs creaked when he crawled onto the bed. After-meal sleeps were the best. He slept during the day because he found it difficult to sleep at night. He drifted off.

Something woke him and he raised his head. His cell door was wide open and the skinny one crept towards him with a wooden club partially concealed behind his back. The bushy-bearded fat one carried wrist straps, chains, and locks.

"Don't move!" the skinny one said. He circled to Lundy's left and shielded the club with his body. The bushy-bearded fat one advanced on his right.

The skinny one lifted the club and poked Lundy in the chest. Lundy grabbed the club and pulled the skinny one towards him. He felt the strain and the skinny one braced his foot on the bed and pulled harder. Lundy released his grip and the skinny one tumbled backwards and struck his head on the floor. The skinny one felt the back of his head and cursed at the sight of his bloodied hand. Lundy laughed.

Lundy saw the leather strap flash and he felt a sudden breathtaking jolt. The bushy-bearded fat one tightened the strap around his throat.

"Take this, you dumb bastard," said the skinny one and levelled a two-handed blow at Lundy's forehead.

***

Lundy's head hurt and voices were distant echoes, "You can't take him…shackled up…big bruise…the hearing."

Lundy was dragged from a car and was pushed and prodded up a wide stone stairway. His leg shackles made it difficult to mount the steps. A door opened and he was shoved into a small room. His head hurt and he was afraid. The gag, shackles and wrist straps were removed and the bandage on his head was adjusted. He was fitted with a straitjacket and sat on a hard bench between the skinny one and the bushy-bearded fat one.

***

Hon. J.C.Pierrot, Justice of the Québec Superior Court called the hearing to order. In attendance were,

Bad Medicine

George Martin, from Québec's Crown Prosecution Service; the Court stenographer; Police Chief Yvan Lévesque and Inspector Danny Bouvette.

Bouvette liked this particular courtroom. It was very well maintained and the Québec maple furniture gave the room a solid appearance, befitting the weighty matters adjudicated there. Bouvette detected the faint odour of the linseed oil used to polish the wainscoting.

Justice Pierrot nodded to the court stenographer and she readied herself.

"Mr Martin, please give us the short version," said Justice Pierrot.

George Martin cleared his throat and said, "There's a summary on the front page."

Pierrot looked over his glasses, "I've read it, George. However, I want to hear it in your own words for the benefit of the others in the room."

Looking slightly embarrassed, Martin said, "My petition requests a hearing to determine the fitness of a Mr Ernie Lundy to stand trial."

"Is he here?"

"Yes, he's waiting in an anteroom, just down the hall."

"Is he under arrest? What are the charges?"

"Yes, pursuant to a warrant issued by Nova Scotia authorities. There are several criminal charges including murder, kidnapping, assault and fraud. The accused is being kept under close supervision at Montréal Neurological Institute."

Looking at Chief Yvan Lévesque, Justice Pierrot said, "Why didn't you hand him over to Nova Scotia and spare Québec the time and expense of this hearing?"

Chief Lévesque leaned forward, "Lundy is the prime suspect in three murders committed in Montréal. A prominent McGill Professor was one of his alleged victims and, consequently, there is considerable public interest in his case. We think it prudent to keep him here until our investigation of these murders is concluded."

"Do the Nova Scotia authorities agree?" asked Justice Pierrot.

George Martin replied, "Yes, they've agreed pending the outcome of our investigation."

"Has he been identified by witnesses?"asked Justice Pierrot.

"He was recently identified by the daughter of TJ Mathews, a prominent Montréal businessman."

"What is Mr Lundy's mental condition?" asked the judge.

George Martin replied, "Based on information provided by the medical staff at MNI, Lundy had an operation that left him with diminished mental capacity."

Pierrot frowned. "Is this a permanent condition?"

Martin said, "I'm not qualified to say. If you order a psychiatric assessment, the probability of permanent impairment may be determined."

Pierrot said, "Let's get on with the hearing. I've got a full docket that will take me well into the evening. I assume Mr Lundy is ready."

"He's waiting in a witness room, just down the hall," Bouvette replied.

"Bring him in," Pierrot ordered.

* * *

Inspector Danny Bouvette knocked on the door of the small anteroom. The door was opened by Ward 5 attendant, Neal Frost.

"We're ready, bring him in," Bouvette said.

Bouvette stepped aside and Neal Frost and Roy Egerton jerked Lundy to his feet. Lundy had a large bandage on his forehead and he stumbled forward with his chin on his chest. When he got to the doorway, he looked at Bouvette and mumbled something.

When Lundy was seated, Justice Pierrot gavelled the hearing to order.

He looked at George Martin. "Mr Martin, do you have anything to say before I question Mr Lundy?"

Martin gestured to Lundy. "Perhaps I should explain his current circumstances."

"Go ahead."

"Mr Lundy's behaviour is unpredictable and, perhaps, dangerous. In consultation with MNI we thought it best to restrain him for this hearing."

"The straitjacket speaks for itself," said Justice Pierrot.

Justice Pierrot said, "Please have the attendants bring the accused to the small table in front of me, I want to question him."

When Lundy was seated at the table, Justice Pierrot said, "Mr Lundy, I'm going to ask a few questions, do you understand?"

Lundy looked at him and mumbled.

"Do you understand why you are here today?"

Lundy looked around the courtroom but said nothing.

"Are you aware of the charges brought against you?"

Lundy said nothing.

"Do you know what day it is?"

Lundy looked at him and mumbled.

Justice Pierrot looked at George Martin and asked, "Was this man medicated prior to this hearing?"

George Martin looked at Roy Egerton who replied, "No your Honour."

Neil Frost grinned and ran his hand down the length of his rock maple club.

Justice Pierrot said, "I will issue an order for a psychiatric assessment of Mr. Lundy. The order will take effect immediately and will remain in effect for thirty days subject to an additional thirty days extension. The assessment is to be performed by a licensed medical doctor, with psychiatric specialization. This hearing will be adjourned until such time as the Crown Prosecution Service requests continuation, but not later than thirty days from this date.

He gavelled the hearing closed.

Danny Bouvette approached Lundy and the attendants and said, "I'll meet you in front of the courthouse."

Chapter 14 Confrontation

"It's a good thing he's dead," Claire said.

Kathleen replied, "I hope Mike Avila opens the chest, I'm not sure about rib cutting."

"I'm still not used to the smell," Claire said.

They walked into the lab and continued their conversation.

"Who's in the morgue today?" Kathleen asked.

"Let me check," Claire said, and pulled a sheet of paper. "Malcolm Paul and Peter Hegel."

Kathleen said, "We'll have to keep an eye on them, after that trick Malcolm played on you."

Claire said. "He scared the dickens out of me, that ugly thing, all wrinkled and slimy."

Her lips curled in disgust.

"He's resented our presence from day one."

"They think we don't belong."

"Not all of them. Freddie Griffin has gone out of his way to make us feel welcome. Some of them accept us."

Peter Hegel and Malcolm Paul wheeled the cadaver, nicknamed Ebenezer, into the lab. With Mike Avila's assistance, they shifted the body onto the dissection table.

Mike Avila called the class to order and they found their places around the table.

He said, "Professor Lupei will give a brief lecture on the anatomy of the heart. Meanwhile, let's prepare Ebenezer for dissection."

Avila removed the sheet from the body and Kathleen recoiled from the eye-watering stink.

I've got to get over this. I don't want them to think I can't handle it.

Avila laughed and said, "Ebenezer looks a little worse for wear and his personal hygiene needs attention."

Avila pulled a scalpel from a small leather scabbard in the pocket of his apron. "I always carry a scalpel, just in case."

He made two horizontal incisions, one from shoulder to shoulder at the top of the breastbone, and the other below the rib cage. Then, he made a vertical incision and peeled back the skin.

Avila said, "The bone saw, if you please, Mr Paul."

Kathleen angled her head, and hoped her aversion would not be noticed. She wished she could plug her ears to shut out the sound of the serrated metal blade sawing bone.

The door opened and Professor Lupei said. "Let's dissect the heart, shall we?"

"Ebenezer is ready," Mike Avila said, and stood back to make room for the professor.

Lupei examined the chest cavity and the exposed heart and lungs. "Excellent work Mr Avila."

Professor Lupei invited the students to the chalkboard and he sketched the anterior view of the heart and its blood vessels.

"The purpose of today's dissection is to study the interior chambers and valves of the heart," he said, and pointed out the direction of flow and the location of valves.

He concluded his lecture and said, "Mr Avila, I'll leave these students in your capable hands for the dissection. If you need me, I'll be in my office."

Avila stepped forward. "Who's assisting this afternoon?" he asked.

Kathleen looked at Claire who looked anxious.

Kathleen tapped Claire on the shoulder and said, "It's our turn."

Avila supplied aprons and gloves. "Put these on and we'll get started."

Kathleen approached the cadaver, and fought the sick feeling in her stomach.

Lord, don't let me be sick.

She held the scalpel awkwardly and Avila came to her rescue. He guided her hand while she made the incision. She cut fat and muscle to reveal the interior chambers of the heart.

Avila said, "Miss Matthews, if you will make just one small incision…there…I think we can let everyone see what's inside."

He moved aside and Kathleen leaned in.

She felt a poke in her ribs, thought it was Avila, and leaned aside. She froze when the cadaver's hand stroked her cheek. Claire yelped and jumped back. For a second or two, Kathleen was unable to utter a sound. Then loud guffaws and hysterical laughter broke out. Malcolm Paul brandished a string attached to the cadaver's wrist. He laughed and pointed at Kathleen. Peter Hegel and Fatso joined in.

Kathleen, her anger barely contained, turned to him and Mike Avila stepped between them. He held up both hands and said, "Let me deal with this, Miss Matthews."

Kathleen's lips curled in anger, and she pointed her forefinger at Malcolm.

Mike Avila said. "Mr Paul, I heard about the disgusting trick you played in class the other day. Please, no more sophomoric stunts."

Malcolm Paul shot a quick, contemptuous look at Kathleen.

Mike Avila said, "Let's get back to the dissection. Class, gather round."

Chapter 15 Examination

Dr Greg Allen, Director of MNI, passed a document to Dr Merrick. "Read this," he said.

Merrick read it, passed it back, and replied, "It looks straightforward to me, Greg. You're being asked to examine Lundy and provide a professional opinion of his fitness to stand trial."

Doctor Allen stammered, "You,…you don't know the whole story behind this man. He's been a patient here for months and, until recently, we didn't know a damned thing about him, including his name."

"I don't understand. Why are you worried about this?"

"Because, in a moment of supreme stupidity, we operated on him by mistake."

Merrick's eyes widened. "How did it happen!"

"That's another story. We're under critical review by the Québec Ministry of Health because of another botched operation that resulted in the death of a Québec politician."

Merrick said, "What's your point?"

Allen replied, "Lundy is a prime suspect in a high profile murder investigation. The Ministry is bound to find out about his operation if the report reveals it."

"If that happens, what sanctions might result?"

"They could do any number of things. For example, suspend licenses, and/or appoint a new Director."

"With what consequences, aside from the obvious?"

"If the ministry sanctioned us, our reputation would be damaged and our funding would be cut. I've

Bad Medicine

initiated a new clinical trial program involving the treatment of shell shock victims. Ministry sanctions might compel the Canadian Army to withdraw funding."

"You mean my shell shock funding might be taken away?"

"It's possible."

Dr Merrick winced.

Dr Allen leaned forward and said, "I'd like you to undertake Lundy's assessment."

Merrick looked surprised. "Why me?"

"You're qualified. You're a medical doctor with specializations in neurology and psychiatry," Allen replied.

Merrick said, "That's true, but my professional experience is in medical research."

"So much the better. This is an extraordinary situation requiring intelligence and good judgment."

"What about his operation?"

"I can't tell you what to report. However, bear in mind what good you can do for these poor shell shock victims. What do you say? Will you undertake the assessment?"

Merrick replied, "I'll agree to do it on one condition."

"What's that?"

"My report must be submitted as written with no changes."

Allen stroked his chin and looked up at the ceiling. "Agreed."

Chapter 16 Evaluation

"I'm a little early for our meeting," Kathleen said.

"It's a good time, please come in," Dr Merrick replied.

Kathleen placed her portfolio on Merrick's desk. "I've studied your program on shell shock and I can't wait to begin."

"Before we discuss the shell shock program, there's something else I want to discuss," Merrick said.

Kathleen furrowed her brow.

What now?

He said, "Don't worry, the shell shock program will proceed as planned. Dr Allen wants me to undertake a court ordered psychiatric evaluation of a patient and I could use your assistance. Your experience at the Institute will come in handy."

Kathleen felt relief and leaned forward. "I'd be happy to assist."

He said, "Our first session is next week."

She replied, "What will I be doing?"

Dr Merrick handed her a sheaf of papers. "I've developed some evaluation sheets. I'd like you to familiarize yourself with them because I'd like you to take notes. I must give my full attention to the patient and not be distracted by note taking."

Kathleen said, "When and where will the assessment take place?"

"Monday at 9:00 AM at the Institute. I'll meet you in the reception area," he replied.

He stood and said, "I think that's it for now, we've got work to do before next week's session."

***

Kathleen's Apartment

Later that evening Kathleen spread Merrick's papers on her desk and read the Order for a Forensic Assessment. She saw the name Ernie Lundy, and felt a cold chill.

I don't want to do it, but how can I say no?

She called her father to talk about it.

He wasn't much help. "I'll support your decision," he said.

She made up her mind and said," I can't let this stop me. I'll do whatever it takes."

"You're sure it won't bother you to confront Lundy again?" he asked.

"He's well guarded and Dr Merrick will ask the questions. I'm just taking notes. I'll stay in the background. There's a chance he won't even see me."

He replied. "I know how much getting a medical degree means to you but if you feel like you'd like to do something else, your mother and I will support your decision. There's always a place in the family business."

"I'm not quitting, Daddy. Don't worry about me, I'll be all right."

Chapter 17 Ernie

Warren Davies bit into a large apple and asked, "What happened at the hearing?"

Roy Egerton replied, "The judge ordered an assessment."

Davies wiped a dribble of juice from his chin. "Did Billy behave himself?"

"He was all right. He sounded pretty stupid when he answered questions," Neal Frost said.

Davies laughed. "He's no Mark Twain, that's for sure."

Egerton asked, "Has anyone checked on him since you brought him back?"

"I'll take a look," said Frost.

* * *

Lundy remembered the struggle in his cell, driving in the car, sitting in the courtroom, listening to the man.

He lay on his steel frame bed, closed his eyes, and played the memory loop over and over. He struggled to find meaning but was interrupted by a familiar metal on metal scraping sound. Light shone through and he saw the skinny one's thin lips and rotted teeth framed in the meal slot.

"What's up Billy?" he shouted.

Lundy crept closer and looked through the slot.

"Don't give me the evil eye, you moron," the skinny one said. He jammed a finger through the slot and Ernie reeled backwards. Lundy was angry and found his inner voice.

I'm Ernie, I'm not Billy!

He picked up his metal bowl and clanged it off the door. It rolled around the stone floor in ever decreasing circles.

The voice of the skinny one echoed down the hallway. "No supper for you, Billy!"

"I'm Ernie, I'm not Billy!"Lundy shouted. The sound of his voice echoed off the walls.

"*I'm Ernie!*"

He went to his bed and closed his eyes. He wanted to relive today's events but his thoughts scattered like rabbits. He felt confused and fearful and screamed until his throat hurt.

Chapter 18 Body

The door opened and they saw Avila on the far side of the room beside the garage door. An ambulance waited and a body bag lay inside on a stretcher.

Avila said, "We have to get this body into the alcove. Miss Matthews, please go to the storage room and fetch a pair of scissors."

Kathleen turned on light and searched the shelves. She sorted through bone saws, knives, scalpels, clamps, forceps and, finally, scissors. She chose a mid-sized pair of scissors, and gave them to Avila.

Avila said to Claire, "Cut the stitching while I prepare the embalming chemicals."

Claire held the scissors, looked at Kathleen, and grimaced. She angled a scissor blade under the first loop of twine and cut a six inch opening. A sudden puff of gas sent her running to the sink with her hand over her mouth. Several honking coughs later, she washed her hands and splashed cold water on her face. Kathleen followed Claire to the sink.

Claire spat and turned her head sideways. "If this is what doctors have to do, I'm not sure I'm ready for it."

"It's what medical students have to do, at least for now," Kathleen replied.

Avila approached. "Don't worry, it happens to most of us the first time. If you're feeling better, let's go back and finish the job."

Kathleen asked, "Do cadavers always come in stitched canvas bags?"

Avila replied, "Not always, sometimes they're covered with a sheet. It depends on the source. The General Hospital prefers canvas bags and the Institute prefers sheets."

An hour or so later, the cadaver, a woman, was prepped. Her toe tag said she was fifty-six, but she looked older, with matted hair and a care worn face. They placed her body in a cloth-lined wooden box. Later, in the anatomy lab, her innards would be exposed for serious examination by medical students.

Avila said, "It's important to become familiar with the operation of the morgue. Your assignment here is part of the course. Let's walk around and I'll explain things. You may take notes, however, you will not be examined on your knowledge of the morgue."

Avila pointed to a wooden box near the door. "Here's our old friend, Ebenezer."

Avila pulled back the rubber sheet. "He's a little worse for wear now we're half way through the study of his major organs."

"It must be a challenge to keep him preserved for the duration of the course," Kathleen said.

Avila replied, "Cadavers decompose and it's a constant challenge to keep it in check. I don't want to send you rushing to the sink again, however, when the time comes to do the craniotomy, you might expect his brain to be a bit mushy."

Kathleen felt her stomach roll and saw Claire's face turn pale.

"How do you ensure cadavers are fit to dissect from week to week?" Kathleen asked.

"They're washed with a Formalin solution after each lab session and I take special care to ensure decay is nipped in the bud."

Avila picked up a round metal cylinder with a short hose and a pump handle. He pumped the handle and sprayed Formalin on Ebenezer.

He said, "Formalin disinfects and temporarily preserves human remains, it produces the tell-tale firmness of cadaver flesh."

"I'll never get used to the smell," Claire said, wiping tears from her eyes.

"The smell is disagreeable but not its most dangerous property," Avila said. He carefully placed the cylinder under the table. "Formalin attacks mucous membranes, so avoid breathing it or getting it on your skin. It's particularly bad if it gets in your eyes."

Claire asked, "Where do the bodies come from?"

Avila replied, "Hospitals, penitentiaries, jails, orphanages, asylums. The Institute is one of our important suppliers. They seem to have a suicide every month."

Feeling more comfortable with Avila, Kathleen ventured a comment, "I've heard you referred to as Cadman. Where did the name come from?"

Avila said with a smile, "The name has been around for a while. It's short for, 'cadaver man' but the proper term for the person who takes care of cadavers is Diener. The word is derived from the German word Leichendiener, which literally means corpse servant."

Avila looked at the clock and said, "Let's put Ebenezer on the gurney and wheel him to the anatomy lab. We don't want him to be late for his next show."

Chapter 19 Headlines

TJ Mathews padded to the front door in his comfortably scuffed leather slippers. It was past 9:00 AM and he was enjoying his first full weekend at home in over a month. Kathleen stayed overnight and she looked forward to some much needed family time.

Her father returned to the kitchen with two neatly folded newspapers and poured himself a cup of coffee.

"Want one?" he said, gesturing with the coffee pot.

"Yes, please, black," Kathleen replied.

"When did you give up cream and sugar?"

"Since medical school. I drink a lot of coffee and I don't always have cream and sugar on hand. I got used to drinking it black."

He held a folded newspaper in each hand. "Standard or Gazette?"

"I know you like the Gazette so give me the Standard," she replied.

Clad in housecoats and pyjamas, they sat at opposite ends of the table, sipped coffee and spread the newspapers.

She pointed to the front page of the Standard. "The front-page story is about the mayor's new car, paid for by the city."

"The stock market has taken another dive," he grumbled.

TJ turned his attention to the front page of the Gazette while Kathleen searched the Standard for something interesting. She settled for the editorial page and a story that bemoaned the lack of progress in solving the Montréal murders. She lifted her head and looked out the window and thought about her recent encounter with the reporter. He hadn't continued to pester her and, for that, she was thankful. However, she knew that he was pursuing a story and, sooner or later, he would show up.

She returned to the story and was interrupted by a familiar noise. Her father was unhappy about something.

The furrows in his brow prompted her to ask, "Bad news?"

He laid the paper in front of her.

Suspect Arrested in Professor's Brutal Murder, by Jimmy Moyer, Gazette Reporter.

She took a deep breath.and asked, "What does it say?"

"Fortunately, none of us are mentioned by name but you wouldn't have to be Albert Einstein to know it's us he's talking about," he said.

She played with the loose fringes of her bathrobe. "Have you finished reading it?"

"I've read enough to know it's a problem."

"Let me read it."

"Take the front section," he replied, and peeled it away.

She picked it up and said, "I'll take the paper with me, I'm going to take a hot bath."

"Don't tell your mother just yet."

She walked to her father's side and placed her hand on his shoulder. "I'll read it and then we can discuss what to do."

Alone in her room, Kathleen unfolded the paper. The story said that Lundy was charged with the 'kidnapping and assault of the daughter of a prominent Montréal businessman'.

It's me!

Later that day, her father drove her back to her apartment and they agreed, if approached, to say nothing further to the reporter.

★★★

Kathleen's Apartment

Kathleen heard the telephone before she turned the key. Once inside, she dropped her bag and lifted the earpiece.

"Hello."

"Miss Matthews?" said the familiar voice.

"Yes."

"Jimmy Moyer, from the Gazette, we spoke the other day."

Her body tensed. "What do you want?"

"I was wondering if you might tell me more about Ernie Lundy."

"I have nothing more to say."

His tone was apologetic. "I don't understand, I kept your name out of the story."

Her anger spilled over. "Judging by today's story, I'd say you're not to be trusted."

"Neither you nor your family was mentioned," he pleaded.

"I'm not a fool, Mr Moyer. You clearly pointed the finger at me. How many prominent Montréal businessmen have a daughter and a summer home in Cape Breton?"

"I kept my word," Moyer insisted.

"You may play with words Mr Moyer, but the facts speak for themselves. I have nothing further to say, leave me and my family alone. Good bye!"

She slammed the receiver, pressed her forehead against the telephone box, and waited for her anger to subside.

Chapter 20 Assessment

Lundy heard footsteps and the creak of hinges. A familiar high pitched cackle rang off the walls. "Wake up Billy!"

I'm Ernie not Billy!

Lundy swung his legs over the side. Two men slid through the doorway. The skinny one carried a club and moved to his right. The bushy-bearded fat one carried a straitjacket, straps and chains.

"You're on stage again today, Billy, you're going to have your head examined. I'll bet you've got shit and sawdust for brains."

The skinny one poked him with the club. "Kneel," he said, and Lundy knelt.

Minutes later, Lundy shuffled down the hall. The skinny one walked in front and the bushy-bearded fat one urged him forward with repeated kicks to his behind.

***

Kathleen

During her twenty minute walk to the Institute, Kathleen cleared her mind. It was a pleasant winter's day. The temperature was above freezing, the sky was clear and there was no wind. The sidewalks were mostly bare with a few patches of melting snow.

Bad Medicine

She opened the front door felt the rush of warm air. She met Dr Merrick at the reception desk.

"Good morning, Kathleen. Mr Lundy is waiting for us."

Kathleen followed Dr Merrick and kept several steps behind.

Ernie Lundy sat in a chair, restrained by a straitjacket, and flanked by two attendants.

Dr Merrick approached the attendants, and said, "I'm Dr Merrick from McGill University," he gestured to Kathleen, "This is Miss Kathleen Matthews, my associate."

The bearded man stood and extended his hand. "Pleased to meet you, my name is Warren Davies."

The other attendant extended his hand and said, "I'm Neal Frost, we work together on Ward 5."

The attendants sat on either side of Lundy. Lundy turned his head and looked at Kathleen and a faint smile of recognition came and went.

She held her breath.

Dr Merrick asked, "Are these restraints necessary? Is Mr Lundy so dangerous?"

Davies replied, "He's unpredictable which makes him dangerous. It's also standard procedure to restrain Ward 5 inmates when not in their cells."

Frost nodded vigorously.

Kathleen studied Lundy. His face was much thinner and betrayed a pasty grey pallor. His hair was long and tangled and he had the beginnings of a full beard. The scar across his hairline was almost invisible. There was something about the way he looked at her that made her wonder if he remembered.

Dr Merrick interrupted her thoughts. "I want to move the table to the centre of the room."

He said to the attendants, "Please sit behind Mr Lundy."

He said to Kathleen, "Please sit at the end of the table."

Davies objected. "I'm not sure that's safe. We must be close to him in case he gets violent."

Dr Merrick replied, "If Mr Lundy misbehaves, I'm sure you can reach him before he does any serious harm. I don't want your presence to affect him."

The attendants moved, Kathleen took her seat, and Dr Merrick guided Lundy to his chair and sat opposite him.

When he was seated, Lundy looked over his shoulder at the attendants. Kathleen couldn't see Lundy's face but the angry expressions on the faces of the attendants suggested that Lundy provoked them.

She wondered if Lundy was taking advantage of the situation.

Is he playing possum?

The thought sent chills down her spine and she wondered if she should tell Dr Merrick about her suspicions. She decided to say nothing.

* * *

Lundy

Lundy remembered her.

The man sitting opposite him said, "What is your name?"

Hide everything from them.

"I'm Ernie, I'm not Billy."

"What is your last name, your family name?"

He took three or four deep breaths.

"What is your family name?"

"I'm Ernie, I'm not Billy."

"Are you Ernie Lundy?"

"Yes, Lundy."

"Can you tell me your name? Your full name?"

"Ernie… Ernie."

"Your full name? What is your full name?"

"Ernie, Ernie Lundy."

"What day of the week is this?"

Don't know.

"Where are you?"

Don't know.

An anxious feeling overwhelmed him. He struggled to his feet and tried to jump over the table. He hooked his foot, belly flopped and the table collapsed.

* * *

Kathleen reeled backwards. Her chair tipped over and clattered away. She landed on the flat of her back with her pencil still in her hand.

The attendants jumped on Lundy's back. Frost raised his club and delivered several hard blows to Lundy's head and Lundy collapsed.

Kathleen lay on the floor, afraid to move.

"Are you all right?" Dr Merrick asked.

It took several seconds to regain her composure. She grasped Dr Merrick's outstretched hand and pulled herself up. Her heart pounded and minutes passed before it settled down.

Dr Merrick righted the upended chair and invited Kathleen to sit down.

He asked, "Are you hurt?"

"I… I'm all right…"Kathleen replied.

Dr Merrick walked past the flattened table and approached Lundy.

Frost was seated on Lundy's back and Davies hovered nearby.

"You'd better take him back to Ward 5," Dr Merrick said.

The attendants dragged Lundy from the room.

Dr Merrick said, "I'm sorry Miss Matthews, I thought he would behave. Obviously, I was wrong. I hope it wasn't too upsetting for you."

She replied, "I'm all right, I wasn't hurt."

Dr Merrick said, "I'm not sure he's fit to stand trial."

Fit? He's barely human!

Kathleen said, "He's a deceiver, don't let him fool you."

"You saw something?" Dr Merrick replied.

"I'm not sure but you may want to conduct another test. I think he knows more than he's letting on.

"I agree, another test is warranted."

"Would his operation preclude significant recovery?" Kathleen asked.

"Not necessarily, it depends on the extent of damage. Dr Smiff was attempting the operation for the first time and I'm not sure he got it right. I reviewed the operation with him and he admitted he may have botched a critical step. Lundy could recover. The brain is a remarkable organ so we'll just have to wait and see."

"Will he ever be able to leave the Institute?"

"I can't say. I'll conduct another examination and hope for something definitive."

Dr Merrick asked, "Are you sure you're feeling all right? You look a little pale."

Kathleen nodded. "I'm feeling better, thank you."

Chapter 21 Ferret

"You've got a hot story, Jimmy. If you can produce new angles, it could be front page news for weeks," Brian Foster said.

Moyer felt a surge of excitement then, a touch of fear at thoughts of sustaining the story with Gazette's senior editors judging his every word.

This is no time to be weak kneed.

He replied, "It'll take a lot of digging and some late nights but there are new leads to follow. When do you want the next story?"

"Can you give me something Sunday for a Monday edition?"

"If I can get to my sources, I'll definitely have something for you."

"What are your plans? What angles will you pursue?"

"The Professor's drug connections, where he got his drugs and what he did with them."

Foster said, "What about the Lundy connection with the Matthews' woman, the daughter?"

"She didn't like the first story and she's very angry. She refused to talk to me."

"If not her, what angle <u>will</u> you pursue?"

"I like the drug angle. I'll get to the Matthews' story later. I'll give her some time to cool off."

"It's your call, Jimmy, but give me something I can print on Monday."

Moyer said, "Last time we met you mentioned a confidential source with inside knowledge about the West End Gang. I've got a story half written and if I could talk to your source, I'll have a good story for you."

Foster replied, "Do you want to meet him tonight?"

"The sooner the better."

"I'll set up a meeting at O'Reilly's. I'll call you at home to confirm."

Moyer asked, "How will I recognize him?"

Foster replied, "Stand at the bar and order a drink. Put your notebook and pencil on the bar. He'll approach you and ask you what you're drinking. You reply, 'I'm having a Guinness, would you like one?'"

* * *

O'Reilly's

Moyer stepped up to O'Reilly's bar and ordered a Guinness. He watched the door in the large mirror behind the bar. Just after 9:00 PM, he saw a thin man enter and look around. Then, he felt a gentle nudge in the small of his back.

"What are you drinking, my friend?" said a gravelly voice, in a half whisper.

Moyer turned to see a ferret-faced man with an expectant grin. The man leaned against the bar and fingered a grimy-green bandanna that looped his neck.

"I'm having a Guinness, would you like one?" said Moyer.

"I thought you'd never ask," said the Ferret, and licked his lips.

Moyer ordered two pints and gestured to an empty table in the far corner. The Ferret sucked foam from the top of his pint and walked ahead of Moyer towards the table. He looked around before he sat down.

When they were seated, Moyer said, "You've met my boss at the Gazette."

The Ferret nodded.

"I don't need to know your name, your identity is safe with me."

"You have the money?"

Moyer slid the envelope across the table. Ferret counted out ten dollars and jammed it into his pocket.

"You know Bernie Landry?" asked Moyer.

The Ferret nodded.

"How do you know him?"

The Ferret took a sip and said, "The West End Gang, the Port."

"What can you tell me about him?"

"He showed up at the Port one day, all new and ambitious. Mattick took a shine to him right off."

"Was he recruited into the West End Gang?"

"Yes. Mattick invited him to meet Gunny Ryan at the Dundrum club. I was there. Gunny liked him and, I've heard, so did Gunny's woman, Sissy."

"Did you know his real name was Ernie Lundy?"

"I didn't know it at the time. I found out later."

"How did you find out?"

"Gunny's woman, Sissy, has a sister named Grace. Bernie knew Grace from his days in Nova Scotia. After Bernie got himself in trouble, Sissy told Gunny the whole story... everything. Gunny was furious and now wants Bernie dead."

"He's a suspect in two murders at the port and the murder of a professor."

"Yes, I know."

"Did you also know he's a patient at Montréal Neuro?"

"The nut house?"

"Yes, he's locked up, awaiting trial."

"How did he wind up there?" the Ferret asked.

"I'm not sure. There was a mix up and now they tell me he's got mental problems," Moyer replied.

"If Gunny gets his hands on him, he's a dead man."

"Was he involved with drugs?"

"Yes, he was. When Gunny decided to get into the drug business, Mattick asked him to handle distribution."

"Is that where he met the Professor?"

"Yes. The Professor had a taste for drugs and, when he ran short, he got connected to the West End Gang."

"Is that how the Professor met him?"

"Yes, it is. They met here, at O'Reilly's."

The Ferret drained his mug and wiped his mouth. He gave Moyer a hopeful look.

"Another Guinness?" Moyer asked.

"Twist my arm," the Ferret replied, with a sly grin.

When he returned, Moyer waited until the Ferret took his first sip of Guinness. Then, he asked, "What do you know about the Professor's murder?"

The Ferret's tongue snaked out and cleaned his beer-foam moustache. "He did it, no doubt about it. When the drug deal was done, the Professor flashed a thick wad of bills. Bernie asked a lot of questions and knew that the Professor married into money and lived in a swanky house. With Gunny and the West End Gang after him, Bernie had to get out of town fast. He was broke and, my guess is, the Professor was an easy mark."

"What else do you know about his other escapades?" Moyer asked.

"He worked at the Port and did whatever the West End Gang needed done, smuggling and such. Otherwise, he kept to himself. I heard he had a girlfriend but I never met her."

"The Captain and Mate of the freighter Dominion were also murdered. Do you know anything about that?"

"Not much. Mattick told me Bernie was on the lookout for a ship from the moment he arrived at the Port. I'm guessing he done them both."

The Ferret drained his mug and banged it on the table. "I've told you everything I know. I'm taking a risk just being here. The longer I stay the riskier it gets. If that's all, I'll be going."

"That's all for now. If you don't mind, I may want to meet you again."

"Next time, bring more money," the Ferret replied.

Chapter 22 Notebook

"They're all against us," Claire said.

Kathleen replied, "Not all of them, Freddie Griffin and a couple of others are all right."

"Yes, but Malcolm, Fatso, and Peter are determined to force us out."

"Maybe so, but the rest of the class won't bother us."

"They're certainly not helping. Malcolm's constant needling is getting on my nerves," Claire said.

"Don't let it get to you, try to ignore him." Kathleen advised.

"I can't, he wants me to quit but I can't let them win," Claire replied.

Professor Lupei entered from a side door and walked to the lectern. Following his lecture on blood flow within the brain, they went to the anatomy lab to study Ebenezer's brain.

Near the end of the lab session, Malcolm excused himself. Claire cast a conspiratorial look at Kathleen and picked up his notebook. She hid it beneath her apron.

When the class ended, Claire left quickly but Kathleen lingered until Malcolm returned. She watched his frantic search for the missing notebook with growing discomfort and then she left.

Once outside, Claire pointed to Malcolm's notebook in her briefcase. "That'll fix him. The midterm is in two days and without his notes he won't pass."

Kathleen said, "You must give it back."

Claire frowned. "Give it back! I thought it would make you happy to put one over on him."

Kathleen said, "I understand your anger and, sometimes, I feel it too. But, it's not fair to sabotage his mid term."

"Why not? What about the dirty tricks he's played on us."

"I understand, but you must give it back."

"It's not that simple. How can I face him and tell him I took it? He'll throw a fit. Who knows what he might do?"

"You could say you found it."

"To be honest, I'm afraid of him. I'd rather throw it away than give it back."

"Malcolm has a bad side but please don't stoop to his level. That's not who I am, and I don't think it's who you are either."

Claire set her jaw. "I'm not giving it back. He deserves to suffer the way he's made us suffer."

Kathleen said, "I'll take it back. The longer we wait, the worse it'll get."

Claire pulled the notebook from her briefcase. "It's not a good idea. Give it back tomorrow, make him suffer, just for tonight."

Kathleen held out her hand and wiggled her fingers.

Claire dropped the notebook into Kathleen's hand. "All right, if you insist, but I still think he deserves punishment."

Kathleen took the notebook into the lab. Malcolm's face was twisted with anger as he searched for his notebook.

He looked up and saw Kathleen's extended hand. "Where did you get it! I've been looking everywhere."

He snatched the notebook and pointed an accusing finger. "You stole my notebook. I've a good mind to report you to Professor Lupei."

"I didn't steal it, I'm returning it," Kathleen replied.

He aimed the notebook at her. "Where did you get it?"

"I can't say."

"I'll just bet you can't. You stole it and then got cold feet."

He pushed the notebook closer, almost touching her.

Kathleen gently pushed the notebook away. "I saw it and I thought you'd like to have it back."

Malcolm leaned forward, with a menacing look.

Kathleen held up her hand. "Stop right there! Don't come any closer."

He stepped back. "Aren't you the brave one," he sneered.

"You've got your notebook so calm down."

She walked away.

Malcolm yelled, "You're a thief! I'll get you for this."

When Kathleen emerged, Claire said, "I told you he'd throw a fit. What do you think he'll do?"

"I have no idea," Kathleen replied.

"He's bound to do something. I just hope you don't regret giving it back."

Chapter 23 Call

Jimmy Moyer

He looked at the clock; it was 7:30 AM.

The hiss on the line was followed by a sleepy-sounding voice, "Hello."

Jimmy Moyer said, "Miss Matthews?"

"Speaking," she replied, frosty toned.

"Jimmy Moyer of the Gazette, do you have a minute to talk?"

A breathy huff punctuated the line.

"Miss Matthews?" Moyer repeated.

"What do you want?"

"I apologize for calling you at this early hour but I have a deadline to meet and I'd welcome an opportunity to talk."

"I was in bed, asleep."

Still frosty.

"I'm sorry I woke you, may we talk?"

"What about?"

"Professor Ducharme."

"Why?"

"We're publishing a story about him…his drug use…his murder."

More deep breathing.

"Please, don't!" her voice quavered,

"It's news, I'm a reporter and my newspaper thinks the public needs to know what happened."

"Don't publish rumours!"

"I have facts and I'm giving you a chance to comment."

"I have nothing to say."

"Hear me out."

"I've got to go."

"Please, don't hang up, it's important."

"Very well, I'm listening."

"I have evidence that Professor Ducharme was addicted to opiates and that. Ernie Lundy supplied him and murdered him."

"Who told you this?"

"A reliable source, an insider. He knows all about Lundy's drug connections and his dealings with the Professor."

"What about Professor Ducharme's wife and child? If you publish that story, his family will be devastated."

"Are you confirming my story?"

"I'm confirming nothing, I'm just asking you not to publish it."

"If you confirm what I've just told you, your connection to Ernie Lundy need never appear. You'll be an anonymous source."

"I'm not confirming anything."

"The story will be published without your confirmation but, I feel obliged to tell you that your connection to Ernie Lundy can't be hidden forever."

"That sounds like blackmail."

"It's not blackmail, it's your opportunity to comment."

"I believe in the Hippocratic oath, 'do no harm' whereas, it seems to me, you believe in the reporter's oath, 'do no good'."

"Don't judge reporters too harshly, Miss Matthews. I'm human, and I feel sorry for his family, I truly do. However, I also have an obligation to report the news. Remember, 'the truth will set you free'."

"Fine words Mr. Moyer, very fine words. However, in your zeal for the story you'll hurt innocent people and, in my opinion, it trumps any obligation to publish what you call 'news'."

Moyer said," I just want-"

The line went dead.

Jimmy Moyer experienced a moment of disappointment but realized that Kathleen Matthews confirmed his story.

Chapter 24 Elvira

Jimmy Moyer studied the Directory listing in the foyer of the Medical Building.

Dean of Medicine – Professor Harcourt – 3rd floor – Suite 301.

He mounted the marble staircase and entered a long corridor. He read the door signs: Suite 314, 315. Suite 301 was at the far end.

The door to Suite 301 was open, and, from a distance, he saw an older woman seated at a desk. Her grey hair was moulded into in a bun and severely parted down the midline. She was bent over a document as he approached and she didn't look up when Moyer entered.

He cleared his throat and that startled her.

She looked up. "Who are you? What are you doing here?"

"I didn't mean to startle you. My name is Jimmy Moyer, I'm a reporter with the Montréal Gazette and I'm working on a story about the Medical School."

"Professor Harcourt isn't in today. He'll be in on Monday. You might come back then."

"I just wanted to talk with someone who knows something about the Medical School. Perhaps someone like you?"

She replied, "I'm not sure I can do that."

"Why not?"

"I'm Dean Harcourt's assistant. He's the one you want."

He said, "You're in a unique position, Miss....?"

"Bergey, Elvira Bergey, that's spelled B-E-R-G-E-Y."

Bingo! She wants her name in the paper.

He said, "Why don't you help me by answering a few simple questions."

"Are you sure I'm the one to answer your questions?"

He said, "I couldn't think of anyone better qualified to give me what I need."

She said, "If you think I can help, perhaps I can answer a few of your questions."

Moyer put his hand on a chair. "May I sit down?"

She stuffed errant wisps of hair into the bun. "Yes, please do."

"Miss Bergey, I need some history on the Medical School. How long have you worked here?"

She blushed and hesitated in her reply. "I'll just say ...more than ten years."

"Come now Miss Bergey, you don't look old enough to have been here for more than a few years."

I'm absolutely shameless.

She blushed and said, "I know a great deal about the Medical School, Mr. Moyer, more than most people around here."

Moyer asked some innocuous questions about the Medical School and she eagerly provided him with too much information. He pretended to take notes and made an occasional comment.

It's time to get serious.

Moyer bit the corner of his lip and looked at her. "I understand you've lost a promising young research Professor who might, had he lived, been among the greats in McGill medicine."

She pressed an index finger to her lips, furrowed her brow and looked confused. "I'm afraid I don't know to whom you're referring."

"Why Professor Ducharme of course. I was told he was a most promising medical man. I understand he was cut down in the prime of his life through the actions of a madman. It must've been tragic to lose him since he was a devoted husband and father and a pillar of the McGill medical faculty."

Her eyes widened and she vigorously shook her head.

Moyer said, "Am I mistaken in my understanding, Miss Bergey?"

She stiffened and said, "Completely! He was anything but!"

"Perhaps I was misinformed."

She lowered her voice and in a conspiratorial tone, she said, "He was passed over twice for a tenured position and the Dean asked him to pull up his socks. Dean Harcourt was very nervous about Professor Ducharme's opiates research. It turned out to be a mistake, a big mistake."

"Are you saying Ducharme was a troubled man," he asked.

"In more ways than one."

"How so?"

"He wasn't here very long before there were strong rumours he was having affairs with female students. He was quite a charmer, but I had his number right from the start."

"Did you know any of his female students, the ones he had affairs with?"

"It was common knowledge he had a relationship with the daughter of a prominent Montréal businessman."

"What was the nature of their relationship?"

"I don't know, but I have my suspicions."

"What can you tell me about her?"

"I can't tell you her name. She was his research assistant and she is currently a student in our medical program."

"What about his research?" he asked.

"He worked with drugs, opiates, things of that kind. I thought it was disgraceful. "

"What got him into such trouble?"

"He was a drug addict!" she said with a look of smug satisfaction.

Moyer shook his head. "Unbelievable!"

She nodded. "Quite!"

"How did you find out about his addiction?" he asked.

"It was common knowledge."

"Did you have personal evidence?"

Miss Bergey frowned, leaned forward, and said, "He was found on the floor of his office, unconscious, with a hypodermic needle in his arm. He had to be taken home."

"Did you see him?"

"No, his technician found him."

"It must've been quite a shock for the technician," Moyer said.

"The technician told the whole story to Professor Harcourt."

"Were you present at the time?" he asked.

"Professor Harcourt often meets with his office door open. I overheard the entire conversation. There are no secrets between us. He trusts me implicitly."

Moyer pictured Miss Bergey with her ear to Professor Harcourt's door.

"What did Professor Harcourt say?"

"He told me to say nothing about it. Professor Harcourt wanted to protect the reputation of the University. He encouraged Vic, the technician, to keep quiet about it and offered to transfer him to another lab."

"Did Vic take the transfer?"

"No, he stayed on. Professor Merrick took Professor Ducharme's place and Vic Pratt now works with him."

She paused and furrowed her brow. She said, "I assume nothing of what I've just told you will find its way into your story, Mr Moyer."

He offered a reassuring smile and said, "Don't worry. It's what we in the newspaper business call background."

She sighed and said, "That's good. What I've told you is in the strictest confidence."

You can't close the barn door now Miss Bergey, the horses are long gone.

He asked, "What is the nature of Professor Merrick's research?"

"The treatment of shell shock. He has an entirely different approach, no drugs, just Freud's psychiatry."

"It might prove interesting to our readers if I were to get the perspective of the technician to round out my story. Do you think Mr. Pratt would be amenable to a conversation?"

"I don't see why not."

"How and where would I find him?"

"He'll be here on Monday. He works in a lab on the second floor."

"I don't like to bother people at work if it can be avoided. Do you have his home address and phone number?"

Miss. Bergey rummaged in a drawer and removed a file folder.

"There's no telephone number on file," she said. She wrote the name and address on a piece of paper and passed it to Moyer.

"Thank you Miss Bergey. I think a technician's perspective on life and work in medical research at McGill will add an important dimension to my story."

Moyer looked at his watch. "Look at the time! I've already taken up too much of your morning Miss Bergey. Thank you for being so generous with your time and for your insightful observations."

"When will your story appear, Mr. Moyer?"

"Soon, just a few more interviews. Would it be possible to speak with you again if circumstances require?"

She beamed. "Yes, indeed, by all means."

Moyer left with a cheerful goodbye. He bounded down the front steps to the sidewalk with the makings of a good story. Armed with new information about Professor Ducharme's research and with Vic Pratt's name and address, he had another important angle.

He couldn't wait to get to his typewriter.

Chapter 25 Story

"It's 3 o'clock in the morning, come to bed," said Josette.

Jimmy replied, "I've got to get this story written and it's got to be right. Brian Foster wants it today. If I come to bed before it's finished I'll never get to sleep."

Josette patted her bump and said, "I want a healthy baby, I need my rest."

Jimmy finished typing his sentence, stood up and held her in his arms. "I'm sorry. You go back to bed, I won't be much longer."

"Why is this story so important?" she asked.

"My stories have sold a lot of papers and Brian wants more."

"Don't stay up too late."

"I won't be too long."

* * *

The next morning, Jimmy sat at the kitchen table and waited. Josette made toast over an open flame on the stove top. She burned the crust and a puff of black smoke wafted to the ceiling. She blew vigorously on the glowing edge and cut away the blackened crust. He scrunched his nose but said nothing. She brought toast, coffee and scrambled eggs to the table and sat down.

He placed his finished story in front of her. "I'd like you to read it."

She spread butter and blueberry jam on her toast and took a crunchy bite. She chewed her food and looked at his typescript.

"Aren't you going to read it?" he asked.

She swallowed and said, "Breakfast first, read later."

She smiled and forked scrambled egg into her mouth. "I'm eating for two, you know."

Jimmy sagged.

She placed dishes in the dishpan, returned to the table, and picked up his story.

"Take your time, read it carefully," he said.

She peered over the top of the papers, raised her eyebrows and gave him a glassy stare.

He grimaced. "Okay, I get it, but I need know what you think."

"Patience is a virtue, Jimmy."

She's doing this deliberately because I interrupted her sleep.

He scrunched down and watched her face as she read. She frowned here and there, but gave nothing away.

She looked up and waved the first page. "This is very powerful stuff, Jimmy. You'd better be sure of your facts."

"You sound like Brian. Don't worry, I have good sources for this story."

"You're inferring Professor Ducharme's addiction contributed to his murder."

"There were no witnesses to his murder but my sources have made it clear who killed him."

"If you're wrong the newspaper could be sued."

"I'm not wrong and we won't be sued."

"You'll make enemies, powerful enemies. Have you thought about that?"

"I can't do my job and worry about who might not like what I write."

"What about this West End Gang? You've exposed their drug dealings at the Port. What if they retaliate?"

"It can't prevent me from doing my job."

"What about McGill and Ducharme's family?"

"They may be unhappy, but I can't help it."

"Who is this Montréal businessman you've referred to but haven't named?"

"It's TJ Matthews."

"Surely, he'll know it's his daughter you're referring to."

"Maybe so, but I've given his daughter every opportunity to confirm or deny what I've found out, and she refuses to talk with me. She'll have to take the consequences."

"Is that fair Jimmy?"

"I'm not paid to be fair, I'm paid to be right."

"What if you're not right?"

"I am right. If it should ever happen I'm not right, then I'll take the consequences."

She patted her stomach. "It won't be just you, Jimmy. It'll be me and your child."

"I understand and I'll protect you. That's the job I have and the life I've chosen."

"What about the drug experiments at Montréal Neuro?"

"In my next story I hope to deal with it in more detail."

"There's a next story?"

"Yes, Brian wants at least two more stories."

"More late nights!"

"Maybe."

"Don't think I don't support you, because I do. You're a good reporter and someday you'll be a great one. Promise me you'll be careful."

"I promise."

Chapter 26 Sunday

Jimmy Moyer draped his wet coat over the chair and waited while Brian Foster prowled the editorial offices. Foster brought his tireless energy to the position of city editor and was as much a part of the Gazette as the giant presses that clanked and hissed in the basement.

Does Foster have a personal life? A family? How does he do it?

Jimmy's wandering mind was interrupted by the sound of Foster's heavy footsteps on the hardwood floor.

"What have you got?"

Jimmy half-turned and placed his story on Foster's desk.

Foster picked up Jimmy's story and made clucking sounds as he read. Some reporters found this habit annoying and referred to him, behind his back, as 'Chicken Ed'. Jimmy respected Foster and hoped to follow in his footsteps. He wondered what it might do to his personal life. He loved Josette deeply and, with a child on the way, demands on the home front could conflict with his emerging career ambitions.

Foster finished reading, walked around the desk, and placed the story in front of Jimmy. "A good effort but it'll need some editing. It's good enough to get front page placement in the morning edition."

"What needs to be changed?" Jimmy asked.

"You need to boost the credibility of your sources. Say, for example, a source familiar with the activities of the West End Gang and, in the case of your McGill source, you might say, confirmed by a reliable source at McGill University."

"What else?" Jimmy asked.

Foster said. "The affair that Ducharme is alleged to have had with the daughter of a prominent Montréal businessman."

"What about it?"

"I assume you're referring to TJ Matthews' daughter."

"Yes."

"Did you confirm it with her?"

"No, I didn't. But I did speak with her about his drug addiction."

"You'll need to confirm their relationship with her or with another reliable source. The publisher's relationship with Matthews demands rigorous fact checking."

"She's not cooperating. I can't get confirmation in time for publication tomorrow."

"Revise your story to remove the inference. Make a general reference to the relationship and leave it at that. Perhaps, in a subsequent story you can be more specific when you have the facts."

"Are you sure the publisher won't block it anyway?"

"The publisher will support the truth wherever it leads, don't worry."

"Just to be clear, in a future story, you want me to provide identifying details but not name her."

"Yes, so far as I know, the courts have never held us liable."

Foster said, "Make those changes and hand your story to the copy editor."

"I'll get to work right away. When do you want the next piece?"

"Let's aim for the Thursday morning edition. What angles will you pursue?"

"I'm going to turn my attention to his drug experiments and his connection to Montréal Neuro. That's where Lundy's is being held and I'd like to know more about how he got there and how it fits with Ducharme's murder."

"What about the Matthews' connection?"

"I won't pursue it for the time being. If you're looking for a Saturday story I may have something by then."

Chapter 27 News

Troubling thoughts kept Kathleen awake. Lundy's surprising appearance, Moyer's pursuit of a story, and the challenges of medical school came and went in no particular order. Sometime after midnight they disappeared, killed by exhaustion and buried in sleep.

The sound of the telephone roused her. In the first hazy seconds, her fears returned but then consciousness took hold. She jacked an elbow, lifted the toasty-warm bedclothes and felt cold air. The ringing stopped and, relieved, she sank into the pillow.

She dozed but was awakened, again, by more insistent ringing. She lifted the covers, stiffened against the cold, swung her legs over the side, and toed into her fur-lined slippers. She pulled the duvet over her shoulders and trudged to the telephone.

She lifted the earpiece. "Hello."

She cleared her throat. "Kathleen Matthews speaking."

"Kathleen, it's your father. I'm sorry to wake you but it's important."

Every child carries the fear of parental loss and Kathleen's thoughts went immediately to her mother. Her heart pounded and it took time to find her voice. "What's wrong? Is it Mother?"

"Your mother's fine, we're all fine, it's nothing like that."

"What is it then?"

"This morning's newspaper, the Gazette, a story by that reporter, Jimmy Moyer."

Kathleen's relief was replaced by anger. "What's he saying now!"

Why can't he leave us alone?

"Let me read something," her father said.

"Go ahead."

Brace yourself.

"Murdered McGill Professor Used Opiates."

He knows! They know! Everybody knows!

Kathleen took a deep breath. "How could he print something like that?"

"Is it true?" he asked.

"I can't say, I'll have to read it."

"Did you suspect him of using drugs?"

"There were signs."

"What do you mean…signs?"

"I'll have to read the story. I'll call you after class. I have lectures this morning and an anatomy lab this afternoon. I should be back shortly after 5:00 PM. I'll call you then."

"I don't mean to alarm you Kathleen but there are inferences in the story that may affect your reputation."

"I'll read it, then we can talk."

"Very well. Read it and call me as soon as you're able."

"I'll call you later. Say hello to Mother, Goodbye Daddy."

For a few seconds, Kathleen stared at the telephone.

Why this? Why now?

She went into the kitchen to make coffee. The wall clock said 6:45 AM. She thought about her class schedule.

I'll get a paper. I didn't give the reporter much to go on so it can't be too bad.

She pulled a thick wool dress over her pyjamas and stuffed bare feet into her boots. She grabbed a scarf, buttoned her winter coat and pulled her hat down over her ears to cover her fly-away hair. She thundered down the steps just as Mrs. Abramowitz, her nosy first-floor neighbour, opened her door. Kathleen caught a glimpse of a tent-sized nightgown and an owlish face as she flew by.

The sidewalks were slick with wet snow, just enough to make running difficult. She hurried past people on their way to work and dodged steaming piles of horse dung when she crossed the street.

In less than ten minutes she had the Gazette in her hands. She waited until she was outside the news stand and on the sidewalk before she opened it. On the left-hand side, two columns wide, she read **Murdered McGill Professor Addicted.** She dug into the story and discovered, somehow, Jimmy Moyer had the story of Professor Ducharme's drug use.

A reliable source at McGill. Who?

It said the police had a suspect in Professor Ducharme's murder as well as the murderer of two seamen. It also stated the suspect was a likely supplier of drugs and robbery was the motive for Professor Ducharme's murder.

I'll bet it will cause a stir at McGill.

She read on and frantically turned to the back page of the first section for the. She gasped when she read, "A reliable McGill University source revealed Dr. Pierre Ducharme was something of a Lothario when it came to his relationships with young female students."

No, no, no! Not that!

She felt faint and leaned against the wall for support. Untamed thoughts raced through her mind and she had difficulty breathing. She crumpled the newspaper to her chest and leaned over.

"May I be of assistance?" someone said.

She looked up and saw the shopkeeper on the steps.

"Thank you but I'm feeling better now. I'll be okay," Kathleen replied.

"You're sure."

"Yes, I'm sure. Thank you."

The shopkeeper went into his store and Kathleen turned homeward.

She walked slowly, with head down and the newspaper under her arm.

How could he?

She reached her apartment building and felt sick. She moved into the shadow of the steps and retched.

★ ★ ★

Chapter 28 Gang

Gunny Ryan threw the newspaper on the table. "Have you seen this!" he said.

Ferris Mattick looked over his shoulder at his boss.

Gunny jabbed his finger at the paper. "There! There!"

"I don't read the Gazette," Mattick said.

"You'd better read it," Gunny said.

"Why don't you tell me what it says, and save time."

"Oh yes, I forgot, you can't read," Gunny said.

"Funny man!"Mattick replied.

"It ties us to that lunatic, Bernie Landry," Gunny said.

Mattick looked at the paper. "It says the guy's name is Lundy?"

"Lundy's his real name, Landry was his alias," said Gunny.

"That guy, yeah. We had nothing to do with those murders."

"Murders ain't the problem, it's our operations at the Port. This reporter seems to know a hell of a lot about what we're doing there."

"I smell a rat."

"It has to be one of our own."

"Landry... I mean Lundy?"

"Nah! From what I hear, he's a babbling idiot. He couldn't find his arse with both hands. It's someone else."

"Any ideas Mattick asked.

"Well, if I had to guess, I'd say it's either Calum Murphy or Harry Sweeney," Gunny replied.

"I doubt it's Sweeney, I see him just about every day and I know him pretty well. It must be Murphy."

"You'd better find out, and quick. I don't like our operations being splashed on the front page of the newspaper. It makes us look weak, it'll encourage our enemies."

"What about the reporter? What's his name?"

Gunny picked up the paper. "Jimmy Moyer."

"How much does he know?"

"More than he should."

Gunny turned the pages of the newspaper. "It says here, this is the first story in a series. That means he's got more to say. We've got to stop this before it gets out of hand."

"Murphy 's the snitch. Find out what he's told the reporter. If we stop the leaks the reporter has nothing to report."

"Any idea where I can find Murphy?"

"He hangs out at O'Reilly's. See what you can find out."

Mattick pushed away from the table. "I don't know why McAllister couldn't do this."

"Because I'm asking you to do it, that's why."

Mattick grimaced.

Gunny put his hand on Mattick's shoulder. "The sooner we stop this, the better. Besides, I trust you to do it right."

Chapter 29 Long Day

Monday

Following the mad dash to the corner store, Kathleen skipped her usual breakfast in favour of toast and coffee. In between bites, she stared at the folded newspaper and fretted about salacious gossip that might make things more difficult. She had a fitful night's sleep, and woke up unprepared for Professor Lupei's class. She dressed hurriedly, packed her notes and the offending newspaper, and caught the 8:40 tram.

The ten minute tram ride gave her time to think about how she might handle questions about the Gazette's story.

She met Claire outside the classroom. Claire looked at her with a bemused grin and said. "You look a mess Kathleen."

Kathleen touched her head. "Is it my hair?"

"It could do with a bit of brushing, let me help you."

While Claire attended to Kathleen's hair, three students passed by. Billy Turner, nicknamed Fatso, shouted, "Looking for lice?"

The others laughed.

Claire shouted back, "I see a louse, a big fat one!"

Claire finished and said, "That looks better, rough night?"

"I hardly slept a wink. I've been running around like the proverbial chicken all morning," Kathleen replied.

Claire said, "We'd better take our seats, we don't want to be late."

The din rose and fell as students told stories and cast nervous glances towards the side door.

Kathleen whispered to Claire, "I'm not prepared, I didn't have time to study last week's lesson."

Claire whispered, "Scrunch down, hide behind Fatso. If Lupei can't see you he won't call on you."

Kathleen shrank into her seat just as the side door opened and Professor Lupei entered. He walked to the small table beside the lectern and opened his briefcase. He placed a folded copy of the Gazette on the table. Kathleen crossed her fingers and scrunched lower.

Professor Lupei began his lecture and, near the end, he folded his notes and went to the blackboard where he sketched the heart.

He turned to the class, held up a piece of chalk, and said, "Mr Hegel, would you please trace the great cardiac vein, the posterior vein of the left ventricle and the middle cardiac vein to the coronary sinus."

Kathleen looked at Claire and mimed helplessness. Claire slid an elaborately drawn diagram of the heart onto Kathleen's desk. It was an amazing drawing, better than the one in the textbook.

Peter Hegel, with chalk in hand, hesitated in front of the board.

Professor Lupei said, "Now, please, Mr Hegel."

Hegel stood in front of the board with his hands by his sides.

Professor Lupei said, "The chalk Mr Hegel, the chalk!"

Malcolm snickered and drew an admonishing look from Professor Lupei.

Hegel drew a few squiggles on Professor Lupei's diagram, shrugged and turned around.

"I'm not quite sure what you've drawn but it isn't what I asked you to do. I suggest you come to my office tomorrow morning at 9 o'clock prepared to diagram the blood flow in the heart."

Hegel lowered his head and slunk to his seat.

Professor Lupei walked to the table and put his notes in his briefcase. The students assumed the lecture was over and began to pack their notes. Kathleen felt relief and stood up.

Professor Lupei saw Kathleen and said, "Ah yes, Miss Matthews, I hadn't noticed you. I assume you're volunteering to complete the diagram, thank you."

He held out the chalk and beckoned Kathleen to come to the blackboard.

Barely catching her breath she said, "I thought the class was over."

Her admission drew laughter from some of the students.

Professor Lupei smiled and waved the chalk. "Come now Miss Matthews, don't keep us waiting."

Claire Winters whispered, "Show them what you can do."

Kathleen felt Claire's gentle nudge and stepped forward.

Kathleen's photographic memory kicked in and she carefully drew the required blood vessels. She stepped away from the board, handed the chalk to Professor Lupei and returned to her seat.

Professor Lupei studied the drawing and said, "Well done Miss Matthews, very well done."

Kathleen whispered to Claire, "Thank you, you're a lifesaver."

***

Lunch

Professor Lupei's class went well, better than Kathleen expected. With two hours to spare before her Anatomy lab, she went to Cafe´duParc for lunch.

She was surprised to find her best friend, Audrie Oakes, sitting nearby, and they shared a table.

"Kathleen, it's been ages," Audrie enthused.

"Too long," Kathleen replied.

"How is medical school?"

"No big surprises. Some men are resentful and try to humiliate us. Other than that, it's going well enough. The academic requirements are challenging but it's nothing I can't handle. I have a good memory and there's a lot to remember."

"Isn't there another woman in the class?"

"Yes, Claire Winters, we've become quite good friends. She's intelligent, tough-minded and not easily intimidated."

Audrie took a bite of her sandwich and Kathleen used the opportunity to change the conversation.

"Enough about my challenges, how about you? How are you doing?"

"I love all my courses, with the possible exception of French. I'm taking two English literature courses and they're both wonderful. There's a lot of reading and writing as you might expect but I'm much better organized than I was in my undergraduate years and I don't find the workload too demanding."

"Are you enjoying your new lodgings? I miss sharing an apartment with you."

"I miss you too, Kathleen. I've got a spacious room and my landlady has given me the run of the place. She allows me to cook in her kitchen and, when it's available, I can use her library. It's a lot closer to my family and mum's home cooking."

Kathleen scooped a spoonful of soup. She sensed Audrie's stare and looked up. "What is it?"

"This morning's Gazette," Audrie said.

Nothing escapes Audrie.

Kathleen said, "The reporter didn't have to say all those nasty things about Professor Ducharme. I feel sorry for his wife and child, they don't deserve this."

"If Lundy is in custody, that can't be such a bad thing," Audrie replied.

"I suppose not," Kathleen said.

"Are you getting questions about you and Professor Ducharme? The news story wasn't very flattering to him."

"Nothing so far. I'm hoping today's story will be the end of it but the reporter is digging for dirt."

"You think there'll be more?"

"Most likely. Lundy has done some terrible things, not just to me but to others. He's a reporter's dream."

Audrie reached across the table and grasped Kathleen's hand. "Do you think the reporter will come after you for your story?"

"He's already tried and I refused to talk with him. Unfortunately, that doesn't seem to have stopped him from getting information from others."

"Are you prepared for the worst?" Audrie said.

"I'm not prepared, there's not much I can do. I thought the worst was being kidnapped by Lundy but this reporter seemed determined to drag it into the open. This could destroy my dream of becoming a doctor."

Audrie reached for Kathleen's hand. "Don't worry, you'll be fine. You can count on me to do whatever I can to help."

"You're a good friend Audrie," Kathleen replied.

* * *

Later

Kathleen stood beside the dissection table in the Anatomy Laboratory. A white sheet covered a large tray.

Professor Lupei used a large diagram to discuss the anatomy of the heart. He said, "In our recent classroom work, we've used diagrams to study the human heart. Today however, you will face reality. Heart dissection is one of the most difficult dissections. Unlike these perfectly symmetrical valentine depictions, real human hearts are misshapen lumps partly covered in fatty tissue. Locating vessels is difficult and depends on your ability to orient the heart correctly. Mr Avila will now show you how this is done." Professor Lupei left.

Avila, peeled away the covering sheet and exposed three containers. He carefully removed a grey lump from each container. The lumps, human hearts, were layered in yellowish-white fatty tissue and looked like small cantaloupes. Two of the hearts were deformed but the third one looked better. Kathleen studied it carefully. She guessed the protrusion was the pulmonary trunk and the wavy bulge angling across the surface was the coronary sinus.

Avila held one of the hearts in his left hand and gestured with his right. "Here are a few clues to help you know left from right."

He pointed out three key features: the pulmonary trunk, the flaps of the auricles covering the top of the atria, and the curve of the entire front side. He drew their attention to the flatter back side.

He rotated the heart and said, "Use your fingers to probe around the top of the heart to locate four major openings."

He walked to the board with the heart in his hand and compared it to Professor Lupei's diagram. He returned to the table and stuck four pencils into the flow openings of the heart. He attached a label to each pencil for, the pulmonary artery, the aorta, the superior vena cava, and the pulmonary vein.

Avila divided the class into three groups. Working in teams, they began the dissection. Kathleen's curiosity overcame her queasiness and she wielded the scalpel with a sure hand.

When the session ended she and Claire went into the hall. Malcolm Paul and his friends clustered just beyond the doorway. Their raucous laughter drew Kathleen's attention. Malcolm stood in the middle of the group holding a newspaper and appeared to be reading it out loud. Kathleen reached for Claire's arm and urged her to leave.

She heard Malcolm say in a loud voice, "It says here Professor Ducharme was sleeping with some of his female students. I wonder which ones?"

Fatso said, "I guess that's one way to get into medical school." Fatso's remark drew an outburst of laughter and guffaws.

Kathleen stopped but Claire tugged her sleeve and urged her to leave. "Just bide your time, Kathleen. Don't give them the satisfaction."

Kathleen and Claire walked away in silence. Kathleen sighed, and shook her head. She hadn't felt this helpless since her ordeal at the Quarry.

Soon everyone will know, what then?

She saw Claire's worried expression and managed a weak smile.

Claire asked, "What's wrong? You look worried."

"You've heard the rumours, haven't you?"

"What rumours? What are you talking about?"

"Those slanderous remarks Malcolm and his friends were hurling at me back there."

"Don't pay any attention to those idiots!"

"Did you see this morning's Gazette?"

Claire said, "I'm a sleepyhead, I barely have time to get washed and dressed for class."

"There's a story about Professor Ducharme. I worked for him as a research assistant and people have made slanderous remarks about our relationship. They're not true but they're hurtful."

"You know the truth. Remember, sticks and stones."

Kathleen said, "I'm afraid things might get worse before they get better."

Chapter 30 Pratt

It was 5:15 PM when Kathleen entered Professor Merrick's lab. Vic Pratt stood in front of an open cupboard.

"Still busy I see," she said.

Startled, he turned around. "Hello Kathleen, I haven't seen you in a while. I'll be with you in a minute, have a seat."

He pointed to a desk in the far corner of the lab.

I don't miss this place.

Vic removed his lab coat, slung it over the back of a chair, and sat down. "What brings you here, this late in the day?"

Kathleen replied, "Have you read today's Gazette?"

She reached into her briefcase and laid a copy of the Gazette on the desk.

Vic looked at the paper and said, "Why do you ask?"

"There's a front-page story about Professor Ducharme. It's not very flattering to him or, for that matter, to McGill."

Vic looked surprised. "How so?"

"You can't be surprised, Vic. The story laid bare every sordid detail of Professor Ducharme's drug use and his murder."

"That's terrible!"

"It's beyond terrible. It also infers he had inappropriate relationships with female students."

Vic shrugged. "I heard the rumours."

Kathleen picked up the Gazette and said, "This story is bound to affect us. I suggest you get yourself a copy of the Gazette and read it."

Vic replied, "I'll do it. What are you worried about?"

"Aside from the attack on Professor Ducharme's reputation, the reported made an inference about our relationship. There are critical comments about our medical research. The story hurts the reputation of the Medical School and the University."

Vic picked up the paper. "How did the Gazette get this story?"

Kathleen pointed to the story. "Somebody talked to this reporter. Somebody who knew about Professor Ducharme's drug use."

He shook his head vigorously. "I hope you don't think it was me!"

Kathleen replied. "I had to be sure. I'm sorry," she said.

Vic's face reddened. "Well, just to be sure, it wasn't me!"

"I believe you and I'm sorry if you felt I was accusing you of anything," Kathleen said.

"A bit of trust goes a long way," Vic replied.

"I'm sorry Vic, believe me," Kathleen said.

"I'm not a snitch. Tell me what's going on,"

Kathleen replied, "This reporter is on a mission. He'll stop at nothing. He might contact you so be prepared."

"I doubt he'll bother with me."

"You never know. Just remember, if he does, speak the truth. Don't repeat rumours or make assumptions about things you know nothing about."

Vic looked puzzled. "I don't understand. What are you trying to say?"

Kathleen exhaled a short sharp breath and said, "Some people have assumed my relationship with Professor Ducharme was other than what it really was. I'll admit we were close and, perhaps, even friends. I cared about him as a friend. That was all there was to it, nothing more."

Vic rubbed his forehead and said, "I know that and I understand. Don't worry about me."

"Who should I worry about?" Kathleen asked.

"Somebody upstairs. Professor Harcourt or Barking Bergey, that nosy, hawk-faced assistant of his."

"I can't believe Professor Harcourt would propagate a story so detrimental to the reputation of our Medical School," Kathleen said.

"I'd believe anything," Pratt said.

"You sound so cynical, Vic."

"You'd be cynical if you were paid the pittance they pay me."

"Is it that bad?"

"Worse, I haven't had a raise in two years. I should be a Senior Technician by now but I'm still a Junior. I rented a larger apartment because my girlfriend wants us to get married. I can barely make rent. I thought I was due a promotion to Senior Technician."

"Have you approached Professor Merrick about it?"

"Yes, but he said those decisions were made by Harcourt."

"Did you approach him?"

"Yes, and he told me there was no money in the budget."

"That sounds like a feeble excuse," Kathleen said.

"It is. When I challenged him, he told me if I need more money I should get a job somewhere else."

"What are you going to do?"

"I'm thinking about working weekends. A friend of my father owns a small cartage company. He's offered me weekend work, moving freight."

"That's hard physical labour. Are you sure?"

"I have to do something. My girlfriend won't wait forever."

"Why not talk to Harcourt again? Explain your situation."

"He wouldn't listen to me last time. I might have been a piece of gum stuck to his shoe."

Vic's bitterness spilled out and Kathleen felt uncomfortable. She decided to escape the conversation. "I have to get home. I've a big assignment to submit and I'm way behind. I hope you get that promotion."

Chapter 31 Perspective

Shortly after 8:00 PM Jimmy Moyer entered a two-story house at 14 Rue Peel. He walked up one flight of stairs and knocked on the door of Apartment B.

The door opened, and revealed a boyish-looking face, topped by a shock of light brown hair.

"Yes?"

"Mr Vic Pratt?"

"That's me."

"I'm with the Montréal Gazette."

"I'm not interested…thank you," Pratt said, and closed the door.

Moyer knocked again. The door opened and Pratt looked annoyed. "I've already told you…"

Moyer jammed his foot in the door opening. "My name is Jimmy Moyer, I'm a reporter and I'd like to speak with you."

Pratt widened the opening. "What about?"

"Your work with Professor Ducharme at McGill."

"I have nothing to say."

Moyer said, "I believe you have a unique perspective on Professor Ducharme's work."

"I'm just a junior technician. I work in a lab, mixing chemicals, cleaning glassware, nothing special."

Moyer sensed Pratt's bitter and resentful tone and guessed that he would talk if he were offered the right opportunity and inducements.

Moyer said, "We're talking in the hallway."

Pratt said, "I don't have nosy neighbours."

Moyer said, "Perhaps, but may I come in. If you don't want to talk, that's okay."

Pratt stepped aside and Moyer entered the apartment.

Pratt invited Moyer to follow him.

Pratt wants to talk.

Bad Medicine

Pratt led Moyer down a hallway, cluttered with winter boots, and into an equally untidy living room. To his right, Moyer saw an opening to a small kitchen. Pratt hurried ahead of him and closed two doors off the living room. Moyer guessed one led to a bathroom and the other to a bedroom.

"Have a seat," Pratt said.

Moyer hesitated. Clothing lay on every available seat: pyjama bottoms, a coat, a wrinkled shirt, balled-up socks.

Pratt stepped forward and scooped up the pyjamas. He looked slightly embarrassed. "I'm not much of a housekeeper."

No kidding.

Pratt said, "There's coffee in the kitchen, want some?"

"That'd be nice, "Moyer said.

Pratt was busy in the kitchen and Moyer looked around.

A bachelor's place.

It was in sharp contrast to his own well-kept home, thanks to Josette.

Moyer saw a wood framed photo of a young woman on the mantle.

Pratt brought two stained mugs and placed one in front of Moyer. "You'll have to drink it black, I don't have any milk, cream, or sugar," he said.

"I'm a reporter, I'm used to drinking black coffee, thank you."

Moyer found a clean spot on the lip of the mug and cautiously took a sip.

Yesterday's coffee, warmed over.

Moyer nodded towards the mantle and said, "I couldn't help but notice the photo of the beautiful young woman. Is she your girlfriend?"

Pratt looked at the photo and smiled at Moyer. "She's my fiancée. We want to get married but it's difficult to put aside enough money for the wedding on my current salary.

Pratt replied, "Perhaps I could help you with that in some small way."

Pratt looked interested. "What do you mean?"

"The Gazette will pay you for good information."

"I don't want to say anything that might get me fired."

"Your name will never appear in the paper and nobody needs to know. Our sources are anonymous and carefully protected. You have nothing to fear."

Pratt sat up straight. "How much would you pay?"

"It depends on how good the information is."

"What do you need to know?"

Moyer opened his notebook and scanned his list of questions.

"Was Ducharme a serious drug user?"

"What else?"

"His research projects. What did he do? Where did he do it? Why opiates?"

"What else?"

"What about his relationships with female students?"

"If I tell you what I know about these things, how much will you pay me?"

"I can pay you as much as $20 for good information."

"Do you have the money with you?"

Moyer touched his hip pocket containing his $25 weekly pay envelope.

Do I risk my own money to get this information?

"Yes, I have the money."

"I need you to give me the money before I tell you."

"That's not how it works, Vic, you give me the information and, depending on its quality, I'll pay you, up to $20."

"Money first," Pratt insisted.

"I'll give you $10 up front and the rest if your information is good."

"Give me the $10," Pratt said.

Moyer pulled out his pay envelope, and gave Pratt a $10 bill.

Pratt smiled, folded the bill and tucked it into his shirt pocket. He leaned forward and said, "Ask away."

Moyer took out his notebook and pencil. "Tell me about Ducharme's drug use."

Pratt cleared his throat, took a drink of coffee, and began, "I didn't notice it at first. Then, later on, our supply of opiates got smaller, way out of proportion to what we should have been using for research. I had my suspicions but I kept them to myself. Then one day, I went to Professor Ducharme's office and found him on the floor, unconscious, with a needle stuck in his arm. A vial of our opiate formulation lay open on his desk. That confirmed my suspicions. He was at least a user of drugs if not an out and out addict."

"What did you do then?"

"I removed the needle and dragged him to the sofa. I didn't want people to see him like that. Then, I told Kathleen Matthews."

"How did she react?"

"We went to Ducharme's office and it was pretty obvious he was under the influence. She helped me to bring him around so I could take him home to sleep it off."

"What happened then?"

"She asked me to keep it quiet because it could cost Professor Ducharme his tenure, his job."

"Why was she so protective of him?"

"He supported her research and encouraged her to apply to medical school."

"Is that all?"

"Yes, that's all."

"Was there a romantic involvement?"

"Absolutely not. They were good friends, that's about it."

"You're saying there was nothing special between Professor Ducharme and Miss Matthews?"

"Yes, nothing special."

Moyer found a fresh page in his notebook. "Let's talk about Ducharme's research."

Pratt patted his shirt pocket. "Go ahead, it's your money."

"What do you know about the research program at Montréal Neuro?"

"Professor Ducharme believed opiates could cure shell shock."

"Why the interest in shell shock?"

"The McGill medical school works very closely with Montréal Neuro. McGill has a famous neurological and psychiatric school and Professor Ducharme was an up-and-coming medical researcher."

"What was so important about shell shock?"

"Montréal Neuro is an advanced treatment centre for shell shock victims from the Boer war. Some shell shock patients, mostly officers, were closely related to political figures in Québec and Ottawa. These politicians brought pressure on the military to do something about it and they decided to fund a research program to find more effective treatments and Montréal Neuro turned to McGill for help."

"Why opiates?"

"Professor Ducharme was influenced by European research. He made a proposal and the Canadian military awarded him a research contract. It was a large contract and the medical school and McGill University were quite pleased about it."

"Did Professor Ducharme's treatment prove effective?"

"The program was halted before results could be confirmed and there were problems, especially at the beginning."

"What kind of problems?"

"Suicide. One of their subjects committed suicide following treatment."

"That sounds serious."

"It was serious. Dr Allen, the head of Montréal Neuro hit the roof and Harcourt ordered changes in the program. Professor Ducharme came under a lot of pressure. I think it was around that time he started to use the opiates himself. We developed a new formulation and he decided to test it on himself. At first it seemed like a courageous thing to do but in hindsight it was stupid because it led to his addiction."

"Did opiates prove effective in the treatment of shell shock?"

"Things fell apart before anything could be proven."

"Fell apart? In what way?"

"Professor Ducharme went to pieces. He became irritable, erratic, unreliable."

"Were you involved in his work at Montréal Neuro?"

"I did the lab work here at McGill. Kathleen Matthews did most of the work at Montréal Neuro."

"Did she tell you about the suicide?"

"Yes, she worked there and she told me about it. She was quite worried."

"What was she worried about?"

"Program cancellation would derail her studies and her hopes of getting into Medical School. Damage to Professor Ducharme's reputation would hurt her chances as well. There was a lot for her to worry about."

Moyer lowered his head and wrote furiously in his notebook.

"What do you know about his drug dealings with the West End Gang?"

"Nothing, we kept running short of opiates and I kept asking him to buy more from Johns Hopkins. Our budget was overspent and I guess he turned to someone else for his supply. At the time, I didn't know he was stealing opiates from our supply cabinet and that's why we were constantly running short."

"What brought an end to his research program at Montréal Neuro?"

"Professor Ducharme's review committee voted to terminate the program following complaints from Dr Allen."

"What where Dr Allen's complaints?"

"If I had to guess, I'd say Dr Allen didn't like his patients used as guinea pigs. The suicide was probably a factor because, I heard later, the victim was a relative of a prominent Member of Parliament."

Moyer wrote 'guinea pigs' in his notebook and underlined it twice.

Pratt looked at the small clock on the mantle and said, "I think we've covered everything. My girlfriend will be here soon. I'd like the rest of the money now, if you don't mind."

"Would you mind if we spoke again, in case anything else comes up?" Moyer asked. He took out his wallet and fished out the money.

Pratt carefully watched Moyer's hand movements. "It depends on what you think this conversation is worth."

Moyer counted out an additional $15 and handed it to Pratt.

Pratt took the money, counted it, and looked surprised. "It's five dollars more than we agreed," he said.

"You gave me some good information. I hope you'll agree to speak with me again," Moyer said.

"As long as you keep my name out of this and you're willing to pay, I'll tell you everything I know," Pratt said.

Pratt grinned and stuffed the money into his shirt pocket.

Chapter 32 Improvement

Ward 5

Lundy felt better in the morning but it proved difficult to organize his thoughts. He lay on his bed, closed his eyes, and waited for something to happen. Thoughts appeared and he grew excited. They drifted away like dandelion seeds. Frustrated, he got up and paced the floor of his small cell. When his anxiety subsided, he returned to his bed hoping to reclaim his thoughts. He chased them and they ran thither and yon, like rabbits. He shouted in frustration and his voice echoed off the stone walls.

A voice came from across the hall. "Hey! Boo-boo!"

The bed springs twanged when he sat up. He crept to the door and pushed the slot open.

"Be quiet, I'm trying to sleep over here," the voice said.

"Hey!... Hey!" Lundy shouted through the meal slot.

He crouched down and looked at the door opposite.

The opposite meal slot opened and two eyes appeared, then a mouth with a rotted teeth. The mouth opened. "If your face looks anything like those stupid looking eyes, you're the ugliest man on Ward 5," it said.

Lundy shouted back, "Hey!... Hey!"

"Dumb shit! Is that all you've got to say?" the man said. His slot slammed shut.

A door opened at the far end of the hall and an attendant shouted, "What's going on down there?"

Lundy saw the meal slot opposite open again and the man retorted, "Shut your ugly face Frost, and go back to sleep!"

Lundy heard two sets of footsteps pounding down the hall. He quickly closed his slot and retreated to his bed. Seconds later he heard the rattle of keys and the creak of hinges as the door of the cell opposite opened.

He heard voices, loud and angry. "You're not so smart now, are you, Ripper?" the skinny one said.

He heard the sound of a club hitting flesh followed by angry shouts from the man across the hall.

Lundy received two meals that day but he didn't hear a meal being delivered to the man across the hall. He guessed that he was being punished.

After dark Lundy lay on his bed listening to the shouts of men up and down the corridor. Occasionally, the door at the end of the hall opened and someone shouted, "Shut up down there. Go to sleep or I'll put you to sleep, the hard way."

"Hey! Boo-boo!"the voice said, in a loud whisper.

Lundy got up and opened his meal slot. "Hey!" he said.

"Just so's you know, if I find a way out of here, I'll take you with me," the man said.

Lundy waited by the meal slot but there was nothing more.

Chapter 33 Cal

O'Reilly's

Kevin O'Reilly poured a Guinness and said, "Haven't seen you in a while Mattick. What have you been up to?"

"Nothing special, working at the port," Mattick replied.

"Gunny dropped by a few days ago, with Sissy. They didn't stay long."

Mattick took a drink and wiped his mouth. "Gunny's always on the move."

A customer at the far end of the bar signalled another drink and O'Reilly stepped away.

Mattick rested his elbows on the bar and studied the crowd. He finished his drink and caught O'Reilly's eye.

"Another?" O'Reilly asked.

Mattick beckoned O'Reilly closer. "Looking for Cal Murphy."

O'Reilly replied, "He came in a few days ago but I haven't seen him since. He's usually here once or twice a week."

"Was he alone?" Mattick asked.

"He met some guy here. They sat and talked for maybe half an hour and then they left."

"You know the guy?"

"No, not a regular, well-dressed, with a briefcase."

"Hear anything?"

"No, they took a table."

"Anything else?"

"The stranger asked a lot of questions."

"The police?"

"Not a cop. A salesman maybe. You know, insurance."

"If he comes in again, please call me, here's my number," Mattick said.

Mattick's phone rang later that night, around midnight.

"Murphy's here."

* * *

Later

Mattick was a block away when heard the raucous noise at O'Reilly's. He stepped inside and squinted through blue-gray smoke. Cal Murphy sat with three low-level members of the Gang. Mattick hung in the shadows and watched. Spilled beer, empty mugs, and boisterous singing testified to an evening of revelry. Murphy's voice rose above the din. He bounced his beer mug up and down to the beat of the music and bellowed a chorus of 'Riley's Daughter'.

Giddy-i-ay, giddy-i-ae, giddy-i-ae,

For the one-eyed Reilly.
Giddy-i-ay, bang bang bang,
Play it on your old bass drum.

Mattick slid from the shadows and the man opposite Murphy sat up straight. Worried looks were exchanged when Mattick approached the table. The men grew silent, set their beer mugs on the table, and tried to get Murphy's attention. The song ended, Murphy drained his beer mug, wiped frothy liquid from his chin, and slammed his mug on the table.

Mattick approached Murphy from behind. He was amused by the animated faces that begged Murphy's attention.

"What, what…," Murphy slurred.

Mattick placed his hand on Murphy's shoulder. Murphy wheeled with raised fist.

Mattick grabbed Murphy's wrist. "Take it easy, Cal, got a minute?"

Murphy blinked several times, closed his eyes and grimaced. He stared at Mattick as if squeezing thoughts through thick mush.

He blinked once and slurred, "Mattick… what the devil are you doing here?"

Mattick released Murphy's wrist. "Let's have a little talk."

Murphy stood, wobbled, and walked to an adjoining table. He scraped a chair across the floor. "Can I get you a beer?"

Mattick shook his head. "Not here, let's go outside…"

Mattick gripped his elbow, "Outside, where we can talk privately."

Mattick nudged and Murphy looked over his shoulder. Mattick gave Murphy's sleeve a forceful tug.

Once outside, Murphy wrenched his sleeve from Mattick's grip. "What? What is it?"

"Not here, keep moving."

"What is it?"

"Up ahead, on the right, the garage," Mattick said.

Mattick unlocked the garage door, pulled a chain, and a solitary bulb cast eerie shadows on the wall.

"What kind of car is that?" Murphy's voice quavered.

"A LeRoy."

"Murphy peered into the open top car which was little more than a wagon with an engine. Are we going for a ride?"

"No, just a little talk," Mattick replied. He walked to a small table

Murphy followed, looked from side to side, and nervously stroked his chin. "Who owns the garage?"

Mattick grabbed a chair. "Have a seat."

Murphy stepped forward but hesitated to sit. Mattick placed a firm hand on his shoulder. "Sit down!"

Small beads of perspiration formed on Murphy's forehead. "Can't we do this later. I've had a lot to drink."

Mattick replied, "We're going to talk now because Gunny wants it."

"What's so bloody important?"

"Gunny doesn't like the company you've been keeping."

"The guys I was with tonight are all okay, aren't they?"

"That's not what I'm talking about."

"Then what?"

"A reporter from the Montréal Gazette, that's what!"

"What are you talking about? I don't know no reporter, I swear."

"You met with him a few days ago at O'Reilly's."

Murphy curled his finger and wiped perspiration from his upper lip. "I haven't been at O'Reilly's since a couple of weeks. Someone's made a mistake. It wasn't me."

"You're lying."

"It's the truth, I wasn't there. I ain't met no reporter."

Mattick stepped forward and backhanded Murphy across the face. "What do you take me for? I know you met with a reporter at O'Reilly's a few days ago and, if you want to live, you'll tell me all about it."

Murphy wiped a trickle of blood from his nose. The left side of his face was red and swollen. "I ain't met no reporter," he repeated.

Mattick lifted a machine hammer from the nearby workbench and mashed Murphy's fingers. Murphy screamed in pain and clutched his mangled hand to his chest.

Mattick grabbed Murphy by the hair, and leaned into him. "Start talking, now!"

Murphy stammered incoherently. Mattick withdrew a knife and ran the sharp blade along Murphy's jaw line. Tiny drops of blood soon became a trickle.

"Talk!" Mattick shouted and released his grip on Murphy's hair.

"Okay, okay, I'll talk. But promise you won't do nothin' to me," pleaded Murphy.

Mattick stepped back. "Go ahead, talk."

"Yeah, I met a reporter. I don't know how he found me but he wanted to talk about the murdered professor over at McGill. I didn't say nothing about the gang."

Mattick asked, "Did he ask you about Bernie Landry, or whatever the hell his name is?"

"Yes, he wanted to know who supplied the professor with drugs, and I told him it was Bernie."

The muscles in Mattick's jaw flexed. "You made a mistake, Cal, talkin' to that reporter. Gunny ain't happy."

"Maybe I did but give me another chance. I won't do it again. I did it for the money. I've been with you guys a long time, I'm a loyal member, " Murphy pleaded.

Mattick shook his head. "Can't do that."

"Awww...we go way back, gimme a break."

Mattick put his hand on Murphy's shoulder and said, "Let's take a walk."

Murphy didn't move. He looked up at Mattick. "Are you lettin' me go?"

"Yeah, let's go."

Murphy stood and found an old rag to wrap his injured hand.

They left the garage and Murphy said, "I gotta get home, I'm beat and I gotta do something about this hand."

He raised his bloody, rag-bound, hand.

Mattick replied. "Me too, you go ahead, I'm taking the alley."

Murphy extended his uninjured hand. "Thanks for giving me a break."

Mattick clutched Murphy's hand and pulled him forward. Murphy fell into the knife blade. Mattick's strong upward thrust finished the job.

Murphy's eyes bulged and he sank to his knees. He gasped, "Why?"

"You're a rat and you'll die like a rat, that's why," Mattick said.

Mattick cleaned the knife with Murphy's bandage and dragged the body into the alley.

Chapter 34 Next

Jimmy Moyer bounded down the steps and moved from shade to sunshine with a loose-jointed gait. He raised his face to the sun and felt its warmth. He buttoned the top buttons of his coat against the chill of the late spring morning. He looked forward to summer, still several weeks away.

He thought about his meeting with Brian Foster and new angles for future stories. The Ducharme stories brought his name to the attention of highest levels of the Gazette. The transition from sports to crime was going well. He was on his way up.

He entered the Gazette building and felt the vibe and rumble of the large presses in the basement as they ground out the afternoon edition. The smell of newsprint, ink, and machine oil energized him and he double-stepped up the stairs.

He strode the second-floor hallway and looked into the newsroom. It was a hive of activity. Reporters were at their desks trying to write amid the chaos. Foster leaned over a desk, engaged in conversation with Beth Meekins, the social page editor. Jimmy liked Beth. She had a pleasant personality and knew more about the social hierarchy of the city than anyone else. She dished high society gossip in an entertaining way. A half hour's conversation with Beth was a tonic. Jimmy made a mental note to check with Beth on the Matthews family. Moyer smiled and moved on to Foster's office.

Ten minutes later, Foster walked into his office and dumped an arm load of copy on his desk. In the course of a typical news day, paper piled on Foster's desk, page by page, until, with the aid of a blue pencil, he dispatched it.

"What have you got for me?" Foster asked.

"A source who worked directly with Ducharme just confirmed that he was a drug addict," Moyer replied.

Foster scribbled a note. "What else?"

"The Matthews' woman had a close relationship with Ducharme but my source denied it was intimate."

"Do you believe him?"

"For now…I'll follow up."

"Is that it? That's not enough to carry a story," Foster said.

Jimmy squared his shoulders and said, "Wait for the best part."

Foster exhaled, "Don't play games Jimmy, spit it out."

"The Montréal Neurological Institute."

"What about it?"

More scribbles.

"I'm calling it the 'guinea pig' angle."

"Tell me more…"

"Ducharme tested opiates on Boer War shell shock victims and things didn't go too well."

"In what way?"

"Suicides and worsened conditions because of the treatment."

"Why haven't we heard this before?"

"They covered it up."

"Isn't the professor's alleged murderer, what's his name, locked up there?"

"Yes, Ernie Lundy."

Foster rubbed his chin. "That can't be a coincidence. What in hell went on over there?"

"I don't know. My source says the Canadian military sponsored the research and the shell shock patients were used as guinea pigs to test the drug."

173

"Where does Lundy fit in? Why is he there?"

"I don't know."

"Does your source know?"

"I don't think so. He didn't work there."

"Who did?"

"The Matthews' woman."

Foster checked his notes. "Jimmy, you've got some juicy leads but I need confirmation. If we make unsupported allegations against McGill, the Institute, or Matthews and his family, the publisher will have my head."

"I'll find a source at the Institute."

"What about the Matthews' woman?"

"She's not talking to me, so far."

"Go to the Institute, get the story."

Moyer hesitated, and then said, "It's going to be a great story but I can't meet your deadline."

"Don't worry about the deadline. This new angle looks a lot better but don't waste any time."

Foster raised his head and looked over Jimmy's shoulder. Jimmy turned and saw Assistant City Editor, Dan Savage, with a question on his face.

"What is it Dan?" Foster asked.

"A murder, last night, downtown."

"And…?"

"Do you want to squeeze the story into this afternoon's edition?"

"Only if it's someone important. Who is it?"

"A small time hood named Cal Murphy. Stabbed in an alley, near O'Reilly's."

Jimmy noted Foster's surprised expression.

Foster asked, "Has the killer been caught?"

Savage replied, "Not so far. The police aren't saying much."

Foster said, "We'll need more details. We won't publish anything today, maybe tomorrow."

Savage nodded and left.

Foster said to Jimmy, "Recognize the name?"

"No, why?"

"The source at O'Reilly's."

Jimmy furrowed his brow. "The Ferret?"

"That's right; you didn't know his real name. He's been a source of ours on West End Gang activities for the best part of a year."

"What happened to him?"

"Three guesses, first two don't count," Foster replied.

"The Gang caught up with him?"

"That'd be my guess."

"The poor bugger, all for a few measly bucks. How could he be that stupid?"

"Despite what pulp fiction would have you believe, most crooks are stupid."

"I never expected covering a story would risk somebody's life," Jimmy said.

"Get used to it," Foster replied.

Foster looked at the clock. "Let's not waste time talking. I'll delay the story but not forever. Go to the Institute, find out what went on. Bring me a good story this time tomorrow."

"I'm on my way," Moyer said.

***

Chapter 35 Recovery

Although the Gazette story caused some embarrassment, Kathleen's worst fears did not materialize. The gibes of her fellow medical students notwithstanding, the gossip at McGill focused on Professor Ducharme's addiction.

She tapped on Professor Merrick's door and responded to his 'come in'.

He put down his pen and said, "A timely visit, Miss Matthews, I've been meaning to talk with you."

Kathleen replied, "Sorry for interrupting. I want to discuss my research program."

"Let's do that, but first let me tell you about my recent meeting with Ernie Lundy at the Institute."

Kathleen was surprised. A conversation about Lundy was the furthest thing from her mind, and about as welcome as a bee sting.

Merrick said, "I met Lundy yesterday. I continued the assessment in his cell. They had his wrists strapped to bed rails but I insisted on their removal. There were some objections from the attendants but I prevailed."

Kathleen interjected, "He's a violent man, weren't you concerned about your safety?"

"I was a bit nervous but I wanted to eliminate the negative influence of the attendants. On our previous visit the tension between Lundy and the attendants, particularly Frost, was palpable."

"I'm guessing you weren't attacked," Kathleen said.

"The conversation was peaceful but his answers seemed contrived."

"I don't understand. Contrived? In what way?"

"Like he was playing dumb, trying to fool me. I think he's smarter than he lets on."

"I suspected as much from our earlier encounter," she said.

"What are you going to say in your report?" Kathleen asked.

"I think he's recovering."

"Recovering? I thought his operation was irreversible. How much recovery is possible?"

"Some patients have partially recovered and the literature reports a few cases of complete recovery. Despite what most people think, the brain appears to be capable of recovery despite severe damage."

Kathleen hid her clammy hands. "Does that mean he will stand trial for Professor Ducharme's murder?"

"I can't say but I wouldn't rule it out. I'll continue to assess him and we'll see how it turns out."

Kathleen felt weak and was glad to be seated. She attempted to speak but the words stuck in her throat. Her rasping prompted Merrick to offer her a drink of water.

She drank and cleared her throat. "I can't believe he might recover. He deserves to spend the rest of his life in a cell, recovered or not."

"That's a bit harsh, Miss Matthews. Everyone deserves their day in court. You know...innocent until proven guilty," Merrick said.

"Perhaps so, but Lundy is evil incarnate," Kathleen said.

"The recent Gazette story certainly made that clear," Merrick said.

Has he guessed my connection to Lundy?

Kathleen rummaged in her case, the better to hide her anger. She asked, "Did you believe everything the paper said about Professor Ducharme?"

Professor Merrick replied, "When it comes to news, I don't believe anything I hear and less than half of what I read. Professor Ducharme had his problems, let's leave it at that."

Kathleen felt relieved, and then thought about Lundy.

Will he ever be out of my life?

She asked, "When do we begin our work at the Institute?"

"The assessment of Lundy has taken priority but I hope we might begin soon. Have you read the outline I gave to you?"

"Yes, I've read it and I've given some thought to the clinical trials."

"Do you have a plan?"

"Yes, here it is."

She placed a document on his desk.

Merrick said, "I'll review it and see how it fits. I'll get in touch with you once everything is cleared with the Institute."

Kathleen asked. "Will that be all?"

"Yes, I'll be in touch."

She stepped into the hall and felt low, weighed down.

Lundy recovered?

Chapter 36 Allen

Montréal Neurological Institute

Jimmy Moyer ducked out of the rain and passed through the front door of the Montréal Neurological Institute. He opened his coat, and enjoyed the comforting warmth of the room. He aimed to fill holes in his 'guinea pig' story via an interview with Institute Director, Dr Greg Allen.

He approached the reception desk. The receptionist's nameplate advertised an absent Miss J. Keeping. He ran his fingers through his wet, matted hair and shivered when a few drops of cold water ran down his back. He heard the click-clack of heels on hardwood and turned to see a young woman coming towards him.

"Good morning," she said, with an eager-to-help look. Her blue eyes were bright and friendly and her mouth formed a half smile. She had a round face, a complete absence of makeup, and light brown hair gathered at the back.

Moyer replied. "Good morning, I'm Jimmy Moyer, I have an appointment with Dr Allen."

She went across the hall to an adjoining office. Moments later a short, round man came bustling towards him. As he walked, the man shoved his free right arm into the dangling sleeve of his suit coat.

"Mr. Moyer, welcome," he said. His right hand shot from an open sleeve. "I'm Dr Allen."

He spoke in a high pitched, lisping, voice and pronounced 'mister' as 'mithter'.

Moyer grasped Allen's clammy hand and said, "Dr Allen, I'm pleased to meet you. Thanks for this interview; I know you're a busy man."

"My pleasure. I'm always happy to have the Gazette take an interest in my work. Please, follow me."

They sat in Allen's office.

"What's it about?" Dr Allen asked.

Moyer fibbed a little, "You're doing groundbreaking work at the Institute and I thought our readers should know about it."

It wasn't exactly a lie, he told himself. He learned to disguise the truth in pursuit of a story. Thanks to Brian Foster's coaching, he understood that occasional misdirection was a job requirement, a reporter's small sin in pursuit of the greater good.

Moyer scanned Allen's office. It was palatial by comparison with the offices at the Gazette. Allen's dark wood desk top was expansive and finely polished, with a deep rich grain. The top was supported by two large, ornately carved, pedestals. A small tray contained monogrammed notepaper.

Allen said, "The finest Brazilian rosewood, beautiful isn't it?"

Moyer nodded.

Allen sat in a leather upholstered chair and, although short, he somehow managed to look down on Moyer. Moyer shot a glance through the knee hole. Allen's chair sat on a raised platform.

Emperor Napoleon.

Allen gestured to an armchair. "Pull up a chair, let's begin."

Moyer settled in and opened his notepad. "I'd like to get some background," he said.

"Go ahead, ask me anything."

Moyer studied Allen's face. His most striking feature was his mouth. It was exceptionally wide and seemed to stretch from ear to ear. His thin upper lip was in sharp contrast to a bulging lower one. His bald dome was framed by grey hair with a few white tufts perched above pointed ears. The combination gave him an elfin appearance.

Moyer posed his first question. "How long have you been Institute Director?"

"Two years this August," Allen replied.

"And before that?"

"I was the Assistant Director for ten years."

Moyer's research revealed that Allen's appointment was highly controversial because of his marginal qualifications and his political connections. In the end, politics trumped competency and Allen was appointed, instead of a much better qualified hospital administrator from Toronto.

Moyer continued, "Which achievements made you most proud?"

Allen swelled like a bullfrog about to croak. "Our neurosurgery program has attracted attention from around the world."

Moyer made a show of note taking. A quick glance at Allen's face told him Allen couldn't wait to tell him more.

While still looking at his notebook, Moyer cleared his throat and said, "I understand your Institute works very closely with the Medical School at McGill."

Moyer caught a look of suspicion.

Allen replied, "We work with McGill in several areas."

Moyer tried to adopt a neutral tone. "Boer War shell shock patients?"

Allen's face darkened. "I… I'm not sure what you mean."

"I mean, has your Institute worked with McGill on the treatment of Boer War shell shock patients?"

A baleful stare and a hard swallow preceded Allen's reply. "We… we… played a minor part in that program … McGill took the lead."

"Weren't these shell shock patients under your care?"

"Technically, yes."

Allen's admission was contradicted by his head-shaking denial.

Moyer watched Allen struggle and it reminded him of a trapped animal.

Moyer continued, "What about the suicide, or was it suicides?"

"Where did you hear about that?" Allen snapped.

"I was told by someone at McGill."

"I have nothing to add," Allen said. He leaned forward with cold, flinty eyes.

"I've been told that Professor Ducharme conducted these tests. Can you confirm it?"

Allen remained tight lipped.

Moyer continued, "Were these experiments successful?"

Allen's face reddened and he looked as though he might burst. "It was all Ducharme's doing! It was a crackpot idea! I shut it down."

Moyer tried to assuage Allen's growing anger. "It seems to me you were right to shut it down."

Allen pressed his hand to his heart. "Yes, I did, thank God. If I hadn't acted we probably would've had even more suicides."

He sat back and looked heavenward.

"How many suicides were there?"

"Just the one, but we had two or three close calls before I shut the program down," Allen replied.

Moyer wrote quickly.

Allen looked at Moyer's note taking and said, "I assume you're not going to print any of this… the families you know."

Moyer ignored Allen's plea and asked, "How many shell shock patients are currently at the Institute?"

"Approximately 20. We can't handle more although the Canadian military would like us to."

"Are you treating them?"

"Yes, the Canadian military will sponsor a new program proposed by Dr Merrick at McGill."

"What's different about it?"

"It doesn't involve opiates, if that's what you're getting at," Allen snapped.

Moyer asked, "Are the results of Dr Ducharme's failed program under investigation?"

Allen crossed his arms. "I can't discuss it. You'll have to take it up with the Ministry of Health."

In for a penny, in for a pound.

"Do you have a patient by the name of Ernie Lundy? I understand he's the prime suspect in Professor Ducharme's murder."

Allen sprang from his chair. "That's enough! The interview is over! No more!"

Moyer persisted. "Is Ernie Lundy here?"

Allen walked to the door and made a sweeping gesture, "Please leave, Mr. Moyer. If you print any of this, I will deny everything."

Moyer placed his notebook in his leather case and, as Allen looked the other way, he snatched a few sheets of Allen's monogrammed notepaper. He paused in front of Allen and said, "We only print the truth, Dr Allen."

Moyer heard Dr Allen's loud 'harrumph' followed by the sharp bang of the door.

Chapter 37 Finagle

Montréal Neurological Institute

Jimmy Moyer was disappointed because his interview with Dr. Allen didn't fill all the holes in his story. He stepped to one side and took out his notebook.

What about Lundy?

He stowed his notebook and returned to the receptionist.

Janice Keeping sat with her back to him, riffling through a filing cabinet. He cleared his throat and she turned to greet him. Her smile was spoiled by a discoloured front tooth and she covered her mouth in a self-conscious gesture.

She averted her eyes. "Mr Moyer, how may I help you?"

She remembered his name, and it impressed Moyer.

Moyer said, "I don't want to bother Dr Allen again, maybe you could help me."

She nodded.

"I inquired about a patient and Dr Allen told me where I might find him but I've forgotten what he told me."

"Do you remember his name?" she said, and reached into the drawer of her desk.

"His name is Lundy, Ernie Lundy."

She turned pages, ran her finger down a list. "Here it is, Lundy, Ernie. He's on Ward 5."

He's definitely here.

Moyer replied, "I was wondering if I might see him."

She looked surprised. "Patients on Wards 4 or 5 are not allowed visitors without the Director's written approval. I'm afraid you'll have to ask Dr Allen."

Moyer fingered Allen's monogrammed notepaper and said, "Thanks, but I don't want to bother him again. I'll arrange a visit on some other occasion."

Moyer stepped away. Then, as an afterthought, he returned and asked, "Where might I find a men's room?"

She gestured. "Behind you… there's a sign… down the hallway to your left."

Moyer lingered in the empty washroom and wondered whether or not he should take the risk of searching for Lundy.

He's a mystery man but he's important to my story.

The door opened and Moyer pretended to wash his hands. Two attendants in blue uniforms stepped up to the urinals. To Moyer's surprise, they left by another door at the rear of the men's room. Moyer paused outside the door until the voices faded. He stepped into the hall and saw an attendant coming towards him. He stepped to one side, and pretended to read his notebook. When the attendant passed, Moyer followed him. The attendant passed through a door with a reinforced window. The sign on the door read,

WARDS 1 to 5
AUTHORIZED PERSONNEL ONLY.

Moyer moved to a far corner and watched the comings and goings of attendants. Most of the time the attendants used a key to open the door. However, when they went to the washroom, they left the door unlocked.

I can get inside, then what?

He took Allen's monogrammed notepaper, crafted a message, forged Allen's signature and slipped through the door. He slipped through the door, climbed the stairs to Ward 5 and looked through the window. At the far end of a corridor, he saw an attendant at a table, engaged in conversation.

Fortune favours the bold.

He pounded on the door and the attendant got up and came towards him. Puffy, sleepless eyes, peered out at him. The door opened and a thin man stood half in and half out of the narrow opening.

"What do you want?" he asked.

What's my alias?

Moyer said, "I'm Jim Moore, a new employee. Starting next Monday, I'll be working on Ward 1. I was wondering what went on up here on Ward 5. Do you think I can have a look around?"

The attendant said, "You're not supposed to be here, Jim. The patients on this Ward are highly dangerous. It's no place for a rookie."

Moyer persisted, "I asked my uncle if it would be okay and he said it would."

"Your uncle!" the attendant scoffed.

"Yes, my uncle, Dr Allen, the Director," Moyer said, leaning in.

The attendant raised his eyebrows. "Do you have his written permission?"

Moyer produced the forged note and was admitted.

Once inside, the attendant said, "By the way, my name is Neal Frost. Do you want the Cook's tour?"

"Yes, I'm particularly interested in your security measures compared to the ones we have on Ward 1," Moyer replied.

Frost said, "This ward occupies an entire floor, unlike the other wards. Each patient is housed in a room, really a cell, of their own. We also have a few isolation rooms so we can handle patients who get out of control."

Moyer asked, "Are the patients isolated from one another?"

"Yes, they're physically isolated and have limited contact with other patients."

"Do you think I could see them?"

"Yes, but I warn you, it can be unsettling for someone who is not used to it. There's yelling, spitting, and sometimes they throw filthy stuff through the meal slots."

Neal Frost unlocked a barred door and Moyer looked down a long hallway with cells, on both sides. Moyer stepped inside and was met with a crescendo of yells, shouts, and screams. They had not gone more than a few feet when meal slots creaked open and eyes peered out.

A shout came from one of the cells, "Yeeeaaaa!… Weasel!… Weasel!"

Frost said, "It's their way of letting everyone know there's an attendant coming."

Moyer wanted to see Lundy but didn't want to raise Frost's suspicion.

"These cells have numbers on the door but no names," he observed.

"There are only twenty cells, but we've never had more than fifteen patients. It doesn't take long to learn who is in each cell. There's no need for anyone else to know, especially the inmates, but they manage to find out who's who, and who's where."

"Are they kept in their cells twenty-four hours a day?"

"Mostly. They can't be trusted outside, they live in the cells."

"Where do they… well… you know… take a crap?"

Frost wrinkled his nose. "In the cells. Removing the slop buckets is something Ward 5 attendants have to do. Nobody likes it."

"How long have you been working on Ward 5?"

"A couple of years. I've been after a transfer for the last six months but it's slow in coming. Nobody wants Ward 5."

"You must have some dangerous men here?"

"Indeed we do. One of them is The Montréal Ripper. His real name is Waldo Speight. He murdered several prostitutes and people compared him to England's famous Ripper."

"You'd think they'd have hung him."

"You'd think. However, he had connections and a good lawyer and he got off by pleading insanity. He'll never get out."

"Any other notorious inmates?" Moyer asked.

"They're all bad, let's put it that way."

Moyer said. "I read in the newspaper that the man who murdered the McGill professor is here. Is it true?"

"Yes, it's true. In fact, he's here on Ward 5. Cell nineteen, at the end, opposite Ripper."

"Did he plead insanity, like Ripper, to get off?"

"His is a whole 'nother story."

"How so?" Moyer asked.

"He hid here, from the police, and in some stupid mix-up, he was mistaken for a surgery patient. He came out a babbling boob but nobody knew who he was, least of all him. He seemed harmless and they put him on Ward 1. However, he turned violent and almost killed a fellow patient. They brought him to Ward 5 until they could figure things out."

"Did they figure things out?"

"Yes, eventually. The police got involved and Billy Boo Boo was eventually identified as Ernie Lundy."

"Will he be put on trial?"

"They're still trying to figure out what to do with him. The police have been here a few times and a McGill professor has had sessions with him."

Moyer asked, "Do you think I could see him?"

"What's to see? Why?"

"Just curious. I'd like to know what a man like him looks like."

"I'll give you a peek through his meal slot. Most of the time these guys are just curled up on their beds so there's not much to see. Don't be disappointed if all you see is a lump under a blanket."

"I understand."

Frost looked through the meal slot and said, "He's not on his bed, I don't see him. If these guys suspect you're going to look in at them, they sometimes-"

Frost yelped, and stumbled backwards. "My eyes!… my eyes!… my fuckin' eyes!" he yelled. He ripped at his shirt, buttons went flying, and he rubbed his eyes with his shirt tail.

"What happened!"

"The bastard hit me with a handful of piss," Frost explained.

Moyer, ever curious, approached the slot.

"Get away from there. He'd love another chance to do it again. Wait here, I'll be right back," Frost said. He ran down the hall.

Frost returned with another attendant. Each attendant carried leather straps and a wooden club.

"This is your lucky day, Jim. You're going to witness some disciplinary action," Frost said.

Frost banged his club on the cell door and yelled, "You hear that, you miserable piece of shit. We're coming in, so stand back!"

The big man pounded his club on the door. and this stirred the other inmates into a frenzy of shouts and screams.

"Stay here, Jim. This is no place for an amateur," Frost said.

Frost cranked his key into the lock while the big man pounded on the door. They exchanged nods and yanked the door open. The attendants charged into the room carrying clubs and straps. Moyer saw

Lundy. He was dirty, wild haired and disheveled-looking, and he cowered against the far wall. For the next five minutes the two attendants beat Ernie Lundy senseless with straps and clubs. They left him, bound and gagged on a blood-spattered cell floor.

The attendants left the cell, bathed in sweat, gasping for air.

Between snatches of breath, Frost said, "You paid for the Cook's tour but got the big show."

When he caught his breath, Frost ran back into the cell and delivered several hard kicks to Lundy's ribs. "Take that… take that," he yelled with each blow.

Moyer felt sick and fought hard to contain his stomach. Lundy's moans followed Moyer down the hall. The other cells were strangely silent.

In the lunch room, Frost grinned and said, "Is there anything else you'd like to see, Jim?"

Moyer cleared his throat. "I think I've seen enough for today," he said.

Frost laughed and looked at the other attendants. "Jim wanted to experience life on Ward 5. I think it's fair to say he got his money's worth today."

Frost accompanied Moyer to the exit and said, "Put in a good word for me with your uncle so I can get that transfer."

Chapter 38 Plan

Ward 5

Lundy's ribs hurt and the swelling in his nose and mouth made breathing difficult. His head hurt inside and out and he had difficulty remembering what happened. In time, the blood flow slowed and then clotted. He wanted to feel his face but his wrists were strapped together.

It was foolish and impulsive to seek revenge with a silly stunt. So long as the attendants had the upper hand, and it seemed they always would, he would be on the receiving end of their torture. A thought came to him lingered long enough to excite him but then it danced away. He waited and it returned, wispy, ephemeral. The fog lifted and he had but one thought.

Escape!

The thought became obsessive.

Escape!

Chapter 39 Testify

Kathleen looked out the window of the 5:15 PM tram and thought about her meeting with Professor Merrick. His suggestion that Lundy might recover bothered her. During her walk home, a familiar ache returned and she had to limp. Her cane was abandoned a year ago and she dreaded the thought of being forced to use it.

At the entrance to her building a familiar voice greeted her.

"Good evening Miss Matthews, I apologize for my intrusion, but I need to speak with you."

Inspector Bouvette's frame filled the doorway.

In another time and place, under different circumstances, she might enjoy a conversation with him. His presence this evening was, however, another reminder of her continuing torment.

She invited him to follow her upstairs. She shifted her briefcase and a small shopping bag to her left hand and gripped the railing for support. He carried her briefcase which made her climb easier.

Once inside, he said, "I won't keep you long; you've had a long day."

Had she been alone, she would have changed into her pyjamas, warmed up her mother's chicken soup, and gone to bed. She took his overcoat and offered tea in the living room.

He added sugar, milk, and stirred. He took a sip and nodded approval.

"I'll come straight to the point, Miss Matthews."

Kathleen placed her cup and saucer on the side table.

"Just today, we heard from the Crown, via Justice Pierrot, that Ernie Lundy will stand trial for the murder of Professor Ducharme."

Kathleen was shocked and looked away. Her throat went dry and she suppressed a moan.

He said, "I'm sorry to surprise you, but I thought you would want to know as soon as possible."

Kathleen looked at him. "Why isn't he being put on trial for the horrible things he did to me in Nova Scotia?"

"The arresting jurisdiction takes precedence."

"Will he answer for all of his crimes in Montréal?"

"Eventually. For now, he'll be tried for the Ducharme murder because the Crown believes that offers the best chance of conviction. He'll answer to other charges later."

"How strong is your case? Have you found any witnesses to the murder of Professor Ducharme?"

"I'm sorry to tell you that we have no witnesses, so far. The evidence is circumstantial but sufficient."

Kathleen bit her cheek. "Circumstantial?"

"There are no witnesses to the murders. We have witnesses who will testify to his interest in Ducharme's money during a drug deal. Mickey Clancy and his sister will testify to Lundy's physical condition in the hours immediately following Ducharme's murder. We hope Mrs. Ducharme will agree to testify. She can identify jewellery in Lundy's possession following the murder."

Kathleen studied his face, and guessed that he wanted something more. "Will it be sufficient to convict him?"

"It's a trial and anything can happen. The Crown wants testimony about Lundy's Nova Scotia crimes to support their case."

He wants me to testify.

Kathleen replied, "He's not on trial for what he did in Nova Scotia, so how does it help?"

He said, "It's a risk, however, if the judge allows it, Lundy's true character will be revealed.

Kathleen asked, "Is that enough?"

Bouvette replied, "I've spoken with Grace Manion and she has agreed to testify as well."

She said, "The poor woman, almost killed because of Lundy's greed."

He continued, "I was hoping I could persuade you to testify as well."

Kathleen replied, "I don't know. I can't give you an answer today, but I do promise to think about it."

"You can't decide right now?"

"I don't think so. When I came back to Montréal to continue my medical studies I thought I had put my Nova Scotia nightmare behind me. Lundy disappeared and I thought, I hoped, he was dead.

More than anything, I want to be a doctor and if all goes well my dream will be realized. However, these newspaper stories threaten my dream and testifying at the public trial of a notorious killer won't help."

He said, "Help us to put this mad man away once and for all. Surely it's the best way to bury the past."

Kathleen replied, "Do you read the Gazette?"

"Yes, they've taken quite an interest in Lundy, Professor Ducharme and his work at McGill."

"Their interest extends to me and my family."

"I guessed as much."

"This reporter...Moyer, has been interviewing people at McGill and probably elsewhere. They're telling stories that associate me with these terrible events. If I testify at Lundy's trial, it will only make things worse."

"Lundy's trial is months away and by that time the stories will cease to be news."

"I don't agree, the Gazette will cover his trial with gusto."

"Maybe so, but as someone said, the only thing necessary for the triumph of evil is for good people to do nothing."

"I want to help you, Inspector, I really do."

He replied, "If Lundy is not convicted of Ducharme's murder, the Crown will defer trial on the other charges and grant Nova Scotia's request to put him on trial there. Given the evidence and the witnesses, you for example, he will most likely be convicted. Bear in mind you are a key witness and could be compelled to testify. In my opinion, you will testify at Lundy's trial one way or the other. Why not here?"

Kathleen said, "If I testify in Nova Scotia, perhaps the Gazette won't cover it and I won't be subjected to the same degree of publicity."

"I wouldn't count on it. There's great public interest in these crimes and the Gazette has done well by covering them. If the Gazette thinks their circulation will benefit by reporting on a Lundy trial in Nova Scotia they will do so. There are more stories to come, so prepare yourself."

"Are you saying publicity is unavoidable?"

"That's exactly what I'm saying."

Kathleen clenched her hands into fists. "Could I be compelled to testify in Montréal?"

"Perhaps, but I'd recommend against it. Your testimony should be voluntary."

"I hope you understand my situation and why I'm so fearful."

"I understand, nonetheless, I'd like you to testify. You'd be a strong witness for the Crown. You could make all the difference."

Kathleen replied, "I'll think about it."

"I've taken a great deal of your time, Miss Matthews. Thank you for tea. I hope to hear from you soon."

"Thank you Inspector, I'll give you my decision in a day or so."

Chapter 40 Guinea Pigs

"What have you got?" Brian Foster asked.

"You're gonna love it," Jimmy Moyer replied.

Moyer grabbed an empty chair and sat down. He rummaged in his case for his notebook. Foster looked on with a mix of curiosity and excitement. "You've got my attention."

Moyer checked his notebook. "How's this for a headline? **Veterans used as Guinea Pigs**."

Foster's eyes widened. "Sounds like a great headline. What's it about, and how good is your source?"

"Two sources," Moyer replied.

"Details?"

Moyer summarized his meetings with Vic Pratt and Dr Greg Allen. He described Professor Pierre Ducharme's opiate experiments including the army's role, the suicide, and other problems.

"Why did the army sponsor it?" Foster said.

"The army was under a lot of pressure and Ducharme offered a solution that turned out to be flawed."

"Have you confirmed army sponsorship?"

"Not yet. I have the name of a Colonel Parton. I'll get confirmation, but I don't doubt the story," Moyer replied.

"It amazes me how a McGill professor, a smart guy, gets himself and his university into such a mess," Foster opined.

"The University liked the sponsorship money and Ducharme was under pressure to come up with something to prove himself."

"What else do you have?"

"Kathleen Matthews was an associate of Ducharme's and she assisted him at the Institute."

"Have you spoken with her?"

"She won't talk to me."

"Maybe we should name names," suggested Foster.

"You mean Kathleen Matthews?"

"Yes, her, among others."

"Not this time, maybe in a later piece about Lundy. I need to speak with her again."

Foster placed a hand on his brow and squinted at Moyer. "Are you going soft on me?"

"She adds nothing to this particular piece. This story is about the experiments at the Institute. Sure, she participated but she wasn't a key figure. It's about McGill, Ducharme, the Institute, and the Army."

"I don't see why we shouldn't name names. It boosts circulation…people like to know what the swells are up to. However, I'll go along with you."

Foster looked out the window. "You've got some great material Jimmy, the editor will be pleased. Write this up and give me something tomorrow, I'll have it published in a couple of days."

"I've got more if you're interested," Moyer said.

Foster leaned forward. "I'm interested, go ahead."

"I met Ernie Lundy."

"How did you manage it!"

"You'd be better off not knowing," Moyer winked.

Foster rolled his eyes.

Moyer continued, "He's locked up with the criminally insane."

"No surprise there," Foster said.

"I know, but here's the real scoop. Lundy got his head operated on because of some mix-up at the Institute. He has some problems but is improving."

"Will they put him on trial?"

"If they can. The question is, his fitness."

"There's your Lundy story," Foster said.

Moyer wet his lips. "I agree. I've got more information on the West End Gang."

"Let's give the West End Gang some more thought. As we've seen with Calum Murphy, they're a nasty bunch."

"Give them a pass?"

"For now."

Moyer opened his mouth to say something but thought better of it and remained silent. He put his notebook in his case and stood up. "I'd better get to work if you want a story to edit."

"Give me something on the guinea pig angle. We'll publish the Lundy and West End Gang stories later," Foster said.

Moyer was two or three steps down the hall when Foster called out, "Jimmy, come back here. There's something I forgot to tell you."

Moyer stuck his head in the door. "What is it?"

Foster approached him. "The Chronicle published a story yesterday. It was based on our story but with more details about Lundy's crimes in Nova Scotia. They named Kathleen Matthews as a kidnap victim. She may not be aware of it now but she'll find out soon enough."

"That's interesting, maybe now she'll talk to me," Moyer said.

★ ★ ★

Chapter 41 Outrage

The Gazette story hit McGill like a bombshell. Sir John Patterson, Principal, called his assistant. "James, come in here!"

Nigel James, a classically trained scholar, followed his mentor from England when Sir John accepted the position of Principal. James hoped to teach but settled for a position as his assistant.

James leapt from his chair. "Sir John, what is it?"

Sir John removed his pince-nez glasses and said, "This newspaper story is outrageous! They're practically accusing us of murder. I won't stand for it. Get Professor Harcourt over here, immediately."

James bolted from the Administration Building. He left before Sir John unleashed his famously furious temper. He'd been on the receiving end of his anger once before and he didn't want a repeat. Besides, he needed a teaching position, and serving Sir John seemed like the best way to get it.

He hurried across the campus to the Medical Building, climbed the stairs and thought, please Lord, let Harcourt be in his office. He burst into Harcourt's outer office and yelled at a startled Elvira Bergey, "Where is he?"

"He's…not in his office…" she replied.

Before she could explain further, James yelled, "Don't tell me where he's not, and tell me where he is!"

A flustered Miss Bergey attempted to cap her fountain pen and inadvertently stabbed her finger with its sharp point. "He's somewhere in the building…"

"Find him…now!"

Miss Bergey sucked her bleeding finger, fled the office, and hurried down the hall. Nigel James swooped into Harcourt's office, paced around the desk and fiddled with loose pages of Harcourt's correspondence.

James completed several laps and imagined Sir John's growing anger. A few laps later, he started for the door and met a breathless Harcourt in the outer office. Miss Bergey hovered nearby, wringing her hands.

James ushered Harcourt into his office and shut the door. Harcourt struggled to catch his breath and said between gasps, "What…what…is it?"

"Sir John wants to see you…immediately," James said.

Professor Davis Harcourt, Dean of Medicine, had never been 'summoned' by anyone, let alone by Sir John. "What's it about? Why the urgency?" he asked.

"A story in the Gazette has upset him."

"I haven't read this morning's Gazette. Do you know what it's about?"

"No, I haven't read it. We'd better leave now, he's not a patient man."

"I'd like to see the paper before I meet him," Harcourt pleaded.

"There's no time, let's go."

Nigel James opened the door and surprised an eavesdropping Miss Bergey. James ushered Harcourt ahead of him. Harcourt raised his palms and cast an errant schoolboy look towards Miss Bergey. She thrust a copy of the Gazette into his outstretched hand. James pinched the sleeve of Harcourt's jacket and propelled him into the hall. Harcourt chopped James' hand, glared at him, and said, "Bugger off!"

James, taken aback, rubbed his hand and stammered, "Sorry…please…go ahead…Dean Harcourt."

It took less than five minutes to cross the campus. Harcourt read the newspaper as he stumbled along. Once or twice, James had to call out lest Harcourt walk into a hedge or lamp post.

"Go on in, he's waiting," said James.

James opened the door and faced a scowling Sir John. "Dean Harcourt is here," he announced. Harcourt cringed behind him.

"It's about time!" said Sir John, and circled his desk. James stepped aside and tiptoed away.

"James, come back, have a seat."

Sir John gestured to one of two chairs in front of his desk.

Harcourt stood behind the plain oak chair, rested his hands on the back rail and stammered, "I can explain…"

"Sit down Harcourt!"

Harcourt flinched and slid into his chair. James moved to the far edge of his chair to put as much distance as possible between him and Harcourt.

"Guinea pigs! Bloody guinea pigs! What, in God's name, have you been doing over there, Harcourt?"

Harcourt raised a fidgety hand and rubbed the back of his neck. "The Gazette's characterization is a gross distortion-"

Sir John cut him off before he could finish.

"Did you approve Ducharme's work?"

"Yes… but not before giving it a thorough review…"

Again, Sir John cut him off.

"Obviously not thorough enough. I've received phone calls from Richard Paul, Chairman of the Board and from three other prominent members. Mr Paul's son is a medical student at McGill and, based on this story, he might transfer to Johns Hopkins. Needless to say, they're demanding an explanation and have called a meeting of the Board's Executive Committee for this afternoon. What will I tell them?"

Harcourt glanced at the clock and shifted in his seat. "The suicide at the Institute wasn't our fault."

Sir John rose, walked around his desk, and looked down on Harcourt. "What about the other problems? The failure of Ducharme's program to have any beneficial result? Ducharme's illegal purchase of drugs? His drug addiction? Consorting with criminals? His affairs with female students?"

Harcourt slumped in his chair. "I can't be held responsible for what Ducharme did."

Sir John glared at Harcourt with cold, flinty eyes. "Ahh… but you are responsible. Leadership means accountability. You are accountable for what happens on your watch. That's the burden of leadership."

Harcourt looked up. "Do you want me to resign?"

"No, I don't want a resignation, I want an explanation. I must convince the Executive Committee that this institution is in good hands and the so-called 'guinea pig' episode is an outrageous distortion. Give me a one-page summary I can use in the meeting. I want it in my hands by 1:00 PM today."

"I'll try to meet your deadline."

"Not good enough. Do it, period, full stop…without fail."

Harcourt rose unsteadily. "I'd better get started."

"Before you go, let me tell you what I will propose to the Executive Committee."

Harcourt sighed.

Sir John waved a single sheet of paper. "I propose an inquiry conducted by the University Disciplinary Committee. This entire affair will be examined from top to bottom, including faculty and student involvement. I want the Committee to recommend appropriate disciplinary action. Richard Paul, Chairman of the Board, will chair the Committee. Since recommendations made by the Committee will come to me, I must appear to be independent.

Nigel James watched Harcourt crawl away.

Chapter 42 Circle the Wagons

Kathleen couldn't sleep. She replayed last evening's conversation with Inspector Bouvette again and again.

Lundy recovered…testify at Lundy's trial…my dream of being a doctor?

Then she worried about getting through tomorrow on a few hours sleep. Somehow, sleep came.

When her alarm rang at 7:30 AM, she turned it off and snuggled into her pillow.

She rolled over, opened one eye, and was temporarily blinded by a shaft of morning sun.

Good heavens! It's 8:00 AM…I have a 9:00 AM class.

Kathleen bounded out of bed and put the kettle on. At 8:30 AM, munching a piece of burnt toast, she gathered her books and notes for today's classes. She caught the 8:45 AM tram and was five minutes late for Professor Lupei's anatomy class.

She peered through the small window and saw Professor Lupei with his back to the class. He was sketching on the board. She removed her coat, and after a quick check of her hair, she stealthily opened the door and prayed it wouldn't squeak. With her eyes fixed on Lupei's back she held her bum against the door to ease it shut. With her coat under one arm and her books under the other she crept down the centre aisle of the lecture theatre. Heads turned as she passed by. She heard a few murmurs and one or two nervous titters.

Keep drawing Professor Lupei.

The classroom buzz amped up and Lupei turned around but by then Kathleen was safely seated.

Whew! Made it.

The anatomy class was uneventful and German class offered her a chance to relax. When class ended, she was hungry and her stomach protested.

She gathered her books and headed for the door, thinking only of lunch.

When she opened the door, she was surprised to see her father sitting on the window ledge.

"Daddy! What are you doing here?"

"Sir John called a special meeting of the Executive Committee of the Board. I thought we should talk before I go to the meeting."

Her father's face showed deep concern and Kathleen drew closer.

"What's wrong?" she asked.

"We can't talk here, where can we go?"

"I'm absolutely famished, there's a diner near here."

During the ten minute walk from the medical building to the diner, he talked about her mother's exhibit at the Art Gallery and Kathleen's anxiety grew. She prompted him to tell her what was on his mind but the pathway was crowded with students and professors and he suggested they wait.

Kathleen attempted to mask the reappearance of her limp.

He asked, "Is your leg bothering you again?"

"Just a bit, nothing to worry about."

He said nothing further but she knew at some future time he would raise the subject again.

The diner was busy but they found a small table at the back. When their food arrived, he leaned forward and said in a voice just above a whisper, "Have you seen today's Gazette?"

He pulled a rolled up newspaper from his coat and placed it on the table. Kathleen spooned her soup and read the headline, **Veterans Used as Guinea Pigs**. She lowered her spoon into the bowl.

She looked up at him and said, "I don't want to read any more just now. Why don't you tell me what it says?"

He squeezed her hand. "You're not named, so don't worry."

Kathleen exhaled and sat back. "That's a relief, although Moyer is bound to drag me into it."

He picked up the paper and slapped the front page with the back of his hand. "Sir John thinks this story creates a big problem for McGill, and that's what this afternoon's meeting is about. The story accuses McGill, the Institute, and the Army, of negligence. The public and the politicians are very upset about using veterans in this way."

Kathleen shook her head. "The medication was supposed to relieve their suffering. Great care was taken in its application to shell shocked veterans. The suicide was unfortunate but it was not caused by the medication."

Her father leaned forward and lowered his voice. "I understand your desire to defend the work. However, what matters is that sick veterans were used, the experiments apparently failed, and people died. People want an explanation and, maybe, someone to punish."

Kathleen frowned. "Professor Ducharme had the best of intentions."

"Maybe so, but people are circling the wagons."

"What do you mean?"

He said, "What I'm about to tell you must be held in strictest confidence."

Kathleen nodded.

"Sir John has called a meeting of the Executive Committee to discuss McGill's response to the story."

Kathleen's said, "I haven't read the story, so I don't know why Sir John feels a need to respond."

He poked the newspaper. "The story blamed McGill, among others, for what happened. Ducharme is dead, so there's not much they can do to him."

"What about his murder and Ernie Lundy?"

"Lundy's not mentioned. Today's story is about the so-called 'guinea pigs'."

Kathleen asked, "What will result from the meeting?"

"Sir John will ask the University Disciplinary Committee to convene, investigate, and recommend disciplinary action."

Kathleen knitted her eyebrows. "I didn't know McGill had such a thing, what's its purpose?"

"It's very rarely used but Sir John believes it's the best way to get ahead of a howling mob and protect McGill's reputation."

"What will the Committee do?"

"Call witnesses, take testimony, draw conclusions, make recommendations, much like a court procedure."

"What about disciplinary action, punishment?"

"They could recommend disciplinary measures for university staff. That could include censure, denial of tenure, suspension, termination of employment. They could even recommend disciplinary measures for students."

Kathleen sat upright and said, "That sounds ominous."

"Sir John is determined to get to the bottom of it. If McGill's reputation suffers, contributions fall off and his plans for growth will be jeopardized. It means no new science and engineering building, medical facilities, and the cancellation or delay of other important initiatives. No Principal wants that to happen on his watch, least of all Sir John."

Kathleen asked. "What will happen today?"

He replied, "The mandate of the University Disciplinary Committee will be approved and their work will begin."

"Will you be on the committee?"

"Normally, two board members serve on the committee and I am one of the two. However, I may have to recuse myself."

"Why?"

"There's a possible conflict because of your involvement in Professor Ducharme's experimental program."

Kathleen felt a cold chill when she realized what it might mean.

She held his hand. "I didn't do anything wrong, I don't know why the committee would have any interest in me, I'm just a student."

"No one is suggesting any wrongdoing; however, expect to be called as a witness."

Kathleen felt hollow inside. "This is distracting and discouraging. I just want to get my degree and practice medicine. Why do newspapers feel they have to tell these stories?"

He forced a smile. "It's what they do. Dogs bark, birds sing and newspapers tell stories. Don't worry; everything will turn out all right."

He took out his watch. "I have to go. Are you going back to class?"

Kathleen said, "No, I have time. I'll stay and finish my soup."

She watched him leave and turned her attention to her soup - now cold.

Chapter 43 Witness

Cafe duParc - The next morning.

"I didn't sleep well, I'm not happy about having to testify," Kathleen said.

Her father said, "Here comes breakfast."

The waitress brought cereal with berries and milk.

She chased a blueberry around the bowl.

"Kathleen, aren't you going to eat something?"

"I'm not hungry."

"You have nothing to worry about. The Committee just wants to understand Professor Ducharme's research."

"I was his research assistant. I have nothing important to say."

"The Committee thinks you do, otherwise they wouldn't have invited you."

"I'd feel a lot better if you were on the Committee."

"There's a conflict, so I couldn't serve."

"Why is Sir John doing this?"

"He wants to protect McGill's reputation."

"What about <u>my</u> reputation?"

"Don't worry."

"What will they ask me?"

"What you saw, what you did."

"As long as they don't ask me what I think."

"They could ask you anything. You don't have to say anything you don't want to."

"How do I do that?"

"Don't be quick to answer. Stay calm, and think."

Kathleen rummaged in her purse and pulled out the letter. "I got this letter yesterday afternoon. It was hand-delivered to me after class. It seems more like a trial."

"I'm not surprised. Sir John has a law degree and lawyers comprise half the Board."

"It's not fair to ask a student to do something like this."

"You'll be fine, just answer their questions," he said.

Professor Ducharme's drug use? Our relationship?

***

After breakfast, they walked across the campus and entered the Administration Building.

Kathleen stopped at the top of the stairs and asked, "Where's the Boardroom?"

219

"At the end of the hall, on the left," her father replied

The hall was lined with portraits of past Principals and Chancellors. Bearded men, collared, severe-looking, like a parliament of owls.

At the end of the hall she saw a man at a desk. The sign read, **Boardroom.**

Kathleen hovered behind her father.

"Hello, Nigel," her father said to the young man at the desk.

The young man looked at a sheet of paper and said, "Good morning Mr Matthews, please go in. You're seated in the gallery, to your left."

The young man unlocked the door and admitted her father. Just before the door closed, her father gave a wink and a smile and mouthed the words, 'chin up'.

The young man looked at her. Deep creases in his forehead gave Kathleen the impression he was a worrier.

She said, "I was asked to report this morning."

She handed him the letter and, as she passed it, she saw that it was signed 'Nigel James'.

He checked his list and said, "You're to go to the witness room down the hall. When I'm finished here, I'll come down to meet you and the other witnesses."

Kathleen didn't know which way to turn.

He saw her dilemma and said, "Go to the main hall and turn left. There's a sign, you can't miss it."

Kathleen found the room and gingerly opened the door. Mickey Clancy's friendly face greeted her and she sat beside him. She looked around the room and nodded to Dr Merrick and Dean Harcourt. She recognized Dr Allen and vaguely remembered the man sitting beside him as Dr Nicholson, a neurologist on McGill's medical faculty. She didn't recognize the distinguished looking man in the business suit. He was in his mid 40's with jet black hair and a well-groomed moustache. His vest was tight around the middle and a sliver of white shirt squeezed over his pants. There was no mistaking Lieutenant-Colonel Parton. His red tunic was festooned with regimental facings, sashes, and medals. He sat erect with his helmet in his lap.

Kathleen wondered who was for and who was against Dr Ducharme. In an earlier conversation with her father, he said Sir John blamed Dr Ducharme and Dean Harcourt for the whole mess.

To pass the time she appraised the other witnesses. Dr Allen probably considered himself too important to be here, wasting his time. The Colonel sat erect with jaw set, bravely enduring torture at the hands of the enemy.

Dr Allen said in a loud whisper, "Confound it, that complete ass, Ducharme, continues to haunt me."

Mickey Clancy leaned closer to Kathleen and whispered, "Ducharme is dead, are they going to dig him up and horsewhip him?"

After a wait of more than an hour, Colonel Parton stood and marched around the room. His restless energy infected the other witnesses. They wiggled, twiddled, and foot shuffled. Dean Harcourt looked worried.

Colonel Parton answered a knock at the door. Nigel James apologized for the long wait. He consulted his list and told Dean Harcourt he would testify first and Dr Allen would be next. Dr Nicholson and Arthur Gray would be called after lunch. Colonel Parton and Dr Merrick were asked to return tomorrow morning. Mickey Clancy and Kathleen were scheduled to testify tomorrow afternoon. Those not testifying this morning were free to leave.

Colonel Parton huffed, "What a load of bollocks!"

Dr Merrick nodded to Dean Harcourt and left. Dean Harcourt followed Nigel James out of the room.

Is it better to be first or last?

Kathleen and Mickey left together.

Mickey asked, "Why all this?"

"The investigation?"

"Yes, the shell shock treatment didn't work and Ducharme has been in his grave for months. What's the point?"

"The Gazette story has apparently tarnished McGill's reputation and Sir John wants to mitigate any damage."

"Why not write a letter to the editor?"

"I don't know, maybe he wants more."

"If he already knows who he wants to punish, why all the rigmarole?"

"White man's justice."

"Meaning?"

"Always give a man a fair trial before you hang him."

They walked as far as the Medical Building and before they parted company Mickey said, "I'll see you tomorrow afternoon."

Kathleen returned to her apartment to prepare. Thanks to a lawyer friend of her father, she had a list of questions to consider.

Chapter 44 Tell Me

Kathleen's Apartment

"Anybody home?"

Her father's voice came from the front hall. She put down her book and hurried to greet him. Her leg hurt. The ache appeared when she got out of bed that morning.

She said, "You're later than I thought, it's almost 7:00PM. Have you eaten?"

"I stopped at the Café."

"Tea?"

"Yes."

He took the armchair and she curled up on the couch.

"What happened yesterday?" Her anxiety was barely contained.

"Sir John cautioned everyone not to discuss any aspect of today's meeting."

She gave him the look she perfected these past fifteen years, and said, "Tell me."

"I'd rather not."

"Was it that bad?"

"Bad enough."

"Were you surprised?"

"A little."

"Tell me."

He poured himself another tea. "Let's talk about something else."

She said, "I've got to prepare for the Committee."

He grimaced and said, "You can't breathe a word of this to anyone."

A flutter of excitement, her curiosity was aroused but she also felt a tightness in her chest. She dreaded what she might hear.

"Tell me," she repeated.

"I can't tell you everything, but I can tell you what I think you need to know."

She urged him to continue.

"Richard Paul will chair the Disciplinary Committee and will question witnesses. He's also Chairman of the Board of Governors.

"Tell me about him."

"He's a top defence lawyer."

"The name sounds familiar. Does he have a son in medical school?"

"Yes, I believe he does. He's mentioned it to me once or twice. Why do you ask?"

"I think his son is in my class."

Her father smiled and said, "That might help you."

Help me? Anything but!

This unexpected revelation bothered her. She drank her tea slowly and, when she finished, tea leaves patterned the bottom of her cup and she studied them.

What does fortune have in store?

She poured herself another cup of tea, settled back and said, "Tell me what happened?"

He cleared his throat. "Dean Harcourt was all but crucified."

"That's awful. He helped get me into medical school. What happened?"

"He approved Dr Ducharme's project and was blamed for its failings."

"What about the others?"

"Dr Allen was very critical of Dr Ducharme. He expected a pat on the back for helping to shut the program down."

He continued, "Arthur Grey, the Vice President of Finance, said Dr Ducharme used University money to buy illegal drugs."

She asked, "What about Dr Nicholson?"

"Richard Paul asked him about the merits of Professor Ducharme's treatment."

"What did he say?"

"He disagreed with the use of opiates. He admires Dr Freud and favours a psychiatric approach."

"So does Professor Merrick," she said.

She continued, "Did Mr Paul ask difficult questions?"

Her father shook his head. "The questions weren't particularly difficult but the way he asked them often implied wrongdoing. It was more like a prosecution than a quest for answers. He adopted a tone of accusation and sly innuendo. It was highly effective and I could see it carried weight with the Committee."

Kathleen asked, "What did he ask Dean Harcourt?"

"He asked about Professor Ducharme's use of drugs. For example, when did he find out about it? What did he do when he found out?

"What did Professor Harcourt say?"

"Harcourt said that he eventually suspected drug use."

Kathleen wrung her hands and asked, "What else?"

"Harcourt admitted that he approved continuation of Ducharme's program after the suicide, and it worked against him."

Her father said, "I'm not sure I should say anything more."

"Please…"

"Harcourt was questioned about Professor Ducharme's alleged affairs with students and why Professor Ducharme was denied a tenure-track position."

Kathleen asked, "What did Dean Harcourt say?"

"He said he had heard the rumours but didn't place much stock in them. He went on to say there were no complaints from students. Harcourt said Professor

Ducharme was denied tenure because his publication rate was poor, among other things. It was a direct attack on Professor Ducharme and, by implication, Professor Harcourt as well."

Kathleen said, "It seems as though I'm appearing before the Spanish Inquisition."

He replied, "I don't think he will be as aggressive in questioning you. After all, you're a student and you simply did what you are asked to do. You weren't responsible for the program and you certainly can't be held accountable for the behaviour of others. Don't worry about it and get a good night's sleep."

He checked his pocket watch. "I promised your mother I wouldn't be too late. I'd better be going."

Kathleen said, "I have to be in the witness room by 2:00 PM tomorrow. Could we meet at the Café at noon for lunch? I'd like to know what went on at the morning session before I testify."

Her father replied, "Yes, I'll leave the meeting to meet you. Stop worrying, and get your rest."

Chapter 45 Intrusion

Following her conversation with her father, Kathleen sat and looked out the window. Mount Royal loomed in the distance. Shortly before 9:00 PM, hunger pangs forced her into the kitchen. She put the day's events out of her mind and busied herself with food preparation. She stood at the stove and stirred a pot of yesterday's chicken soup. The repetitive movement and the delicious smell had a soothing effect.

Her telephone rang and the tension returned.

She lifted the earpiece. "Hello."

"Is this Kathleen Matthews?" a familiar voice said.

"Yes, it is."

"Jimmy Moyer of the Gazette. How are you this fine evening?"

Enjoying my evening…until now.

"I was just about to have my dinner."

She hoped he would take the hint and call some other time, any other time but tonight.

"Do you always eat the evening meal at such a late hour?"

"I eat when I'm hungry. What do you want?"

"I apologize for intruding and I won't keep you. I'm writing a story on the deliberations of the University Disciplinary Committee. Could I get your reaction to today's events?"

Kathleen didn't know what to say. The deliberations were confidential and attendees sworn to secrecy. How could he know what went on inside the room? Maybe he was trying to trick her.

"I don't know what you're talking about," she replied.

"Come now Miss Matthews, I know you've been asked to appear. Your father is on the Board. You must know something about today's events."

"I know nothing about today's deliberations and I have no comment."

"Very well, I'll save my questions for another time, perhaps after your appearance. It's tomorrow afternoon, isn't it?"

"I don't wish to be rude, but it's late and I'm hungry."

"I can be patient Miss Matthews. The Gazette will report the Committee's deliberations. From what I've learned, Professor Ducharme's reputation has suffered another blow. I've been told disciplinary measures aren't out of the question. I hope we might talk again. Meanwhile, I bid you good evening."

He hung up.

Kathleen, motionless, dumbfounded, still had the earpiece in her hand.

Chapter 46 Committee

Kathleen saw her father through the window of the café.

He sat down and said, "I watched you walk in, you're favouring your leg again."

She replied, "I try to relax and think about other things, but I can't help thinking about the Committee. I'll be glad when it's over. Maybe then this ache in my leg will disappear."

He clasped both of her hands. "I know it's hard and I wish you didn't have to do it. I asked Sir John why it was necessary to include you. He said you're one of the few people at McGill who worked with Dr Ducharme every day. Apparently, you're an important witness."

"I don't like the sound of that. If they're determined to crucify Dean Harcourt, I don't want to be his Judas."

He said, "It's not as bad as all that."

"What happened this morning?"

"I don't want to violate the confidence of the Board, but family comes first."

"I know you're uncomfortable, you don't have to tell me everything, just things that might help this afternoon."

"Colonel Parton said Ducharme lied on his application. After the suicide he challenged Ducharme and was told the suicide was not the result of Ducharme's drug treatment. Dr Allen said otherwise. Colonel Parton has been summoned to testify before a parliamentary committee. He is close to retirement and doesn't want to jeopardize his pension. He sounded quite bitter."

Kathleen said, "Dr Ducharme didn't lie. I read his application and it was truthful. Dr Allen just wants to cover up the carelessness of the Institute."

A waitress hovered nearby and he said, "I think the waitress wants us to order something. I'm going to have the soup du jour. What do you fancy?"

"Soup sounds good to me."

They ate, mostly in silence.

When they finished eating, Kathleen asked, "Did Dr Merrick testify?"

"Yes, he did. As you know, he has an entirely different approach. He didn't criticize Dr Ducharme but he disagreed with drug treatment, especially opiates. He favours Dr Freud's approach."

Her father picked up his napkin, dabbed his mouth and declared himself finished. "I'd better be going. We should leave separately so as not to give the wrong impression. When your testimony is finished, wait for me and I'll walk back with you."

***

Mickey Clancy was alone in the waiting room when Kathleen arrived. He frowned and said, "Why so glum?"

She replied, "I have a bad feeling about this, I'd rather be anywhere else."

"You haven't done anything wrong; you've nothing to worry about."

"That only works in fiction. Don't forget, the lions ate the Christians."

Nigel James walked into the room and asked Mickey to follow him.

Kathleen sat alone with nothing to do but think…and worry.

Time passed slowly. She contemplated taking a bathroom break when she heard a knock.

Nigel James held the door open. "They're waiting for you," he said.

Her bladder was close to bursting and Kathleen felt embarrassed. However, nature's call could not be denied and she excused herself. "I'll just be a minute."

She hurried down the hall but couldn't find a ladies' room. A crazy thought ran through her mind.

What if I pee my pants?

She rounded the corner and, much to her relief, a young woman gave her directions.

She left the ladies' room and, moments later, entered the Boardroom to face the Committee.

Nigel James directed her to a chair. Four stern-looking men sat behind a long table in front of her. Nigel James sat at a small table to her right. She looked behind towards the gallery which, she understood, was made up primarily of board members. Sir John wore a stern expression, designed, she imagined, to set the tone. She didn't see her father at first, but looked again and saw him, two rows back of Sir John. When their eyes met, he gave her an encouraging smile.

A voice said, "Miss Matthews, welcome, and thank you for your presence here today."

She quickly faced front. Four sets of eyes looked at her. The man to the left of centre looked at her, expectantly. His face was impassive and his coal black eyes drilled into her. She stammered, "Please...pleased to be here."

Although she clearly wasn't.

Another man spoke up and, having composed herself, she read his nameplate. **Professor Matthew Gardner, Dean of Law.** He outlined the procedure to be followed and introduced the Disciplinary Committee. As they were introduced, Kathleen looked at each man in turn. When Professor Gardner introduced Richard Paul, she froze and fixed her eyes on his nameplate. **Richard Paul, Esquire, Chairman.** There it was in black and white, or rather, black and bronze, Malcolm's father.

She turned again and looked for her father. He gestured and looked as helpless as she felt.

"Miss Matthews, please face the committee."

Richard Paul's voice struck her, cold, hard, and commanding. Kathleen feared the worst.

Chapter 47 Testimony

"Mr James, would you please administer the oath," Chairman Paul said. The Bible looked new, like it had never been used.

While the chairman arranged his notes, Kathleen studied him. Pinstriped suit, younger than her father, hint of a double chin, hair arched upward in front. He looked at her. His eyes were cold, penetrating, dark. She held his gaze and he blinked.

He forced a smile and said, "Just a few questions, Miss Matthews."

She detected a faux British accent.

"I have the impression you were a valuable contributor to Dr Ducharme's work."

"I tried to make a good contribution."

He nodded and Kathleen relaxed.

"Were you his chief collaborator?"

"I assisted, if that's what you mean."

The tension returned and she had an inkling of where he was headed.

"Did he ask you about major changes in the program, for example, new drugs?"

"He kept me informed but he had medical knowledge I didn't have. I'm a student."

Her wariness intensified.

His tone sharpened, "Did you test new formulations?"

"Yes."

"It seems you were a key player in his research."

"Is that a question, Mr Chairman?"

"Miss Matthews, don't be clever. I'll ask the questions."

He shuffled his notes. "Did you have a personal relationship with Dr Ducharme?"

"He was my professor; I was his student, that was the nature of our relationship."

"Did you witness Dr Ducharme injecting himself with opiates?"

I never actually witnessed it.

"No, I did not."

"We've heard testimony that on at least one occasion Dr Ducharme was found on the floor of his office. He was unconscious, presumably as a result of a drug injection. Did you witness this?"

"No."

"This committee has a written statement from Mr Vic Pratt. He said he told you of this."

"Is that a question, Mr Chairman?"

"Don't try my patience, Miss Matthews. Did Mr Pratt tell you about the incident I just described?"

"Yes, but I didn't believe him."

"At some point you became aware of Dr Ducharme's drug use. Is that true?"

"Yes."

"When did you first suspect Dr Ducharme's drug use?"

"Late in the program."

"Did you report your suspicions to anyone in authority, for example, Dean Harcourt?"

"No."

"Why not?"

"I didn't think it was my place to do so."

"You took care of Dr Ducharme after the incident I just described. Is that true?"

"He was my professor. I wanted to help where I could. It was a question of loyalty."

"You knew of his drug use, but said nothing. I'll leave the question of your motivation to the judgment of this committee."

"Did you inject opiates into the suicide victim, Mr Brown?"

"No, I did not. Dr Ducharme did the injection."

"You were there, weren't you?"

"Yes, I was there."

"Did you use opiates on yourself?"

"No, never."

"You must have handled them every day, weren't you the least bit curious about their effects?"

"No."

"Did Dr Ducharme ever suggest testing them on yourself?"

"No."

The chairman gave a skeptical nod of his head and looked at his colleagues. "Let's leave the subject of Dr Ducharme's drug use. This committee has been told you had a most unfortunate encounter with a man by the name of Ernie Lundy. Is this true?"

Kathleen felt her chest tighten and, for a moment, she felt unable to reply.

"Miss Matthews, please answer."

"Yes."

"Did you know Mr Lundy is the prime suspect in the murder of Dr Ducharme?"

"Yes."

"You knew both men, shall we say, very well. Did you introduce them?"

Kathleen's anxiety turned to anger. "I object most strenuously to that question!"

"Your objection is noted, Miss Matthews, however, I insist on an answer."

There was a commotion behind her and she turned in time to hear her father shout, "This hearing is a farce!"

Chairman Paul turned to the gallery and said, "I understand it can be difficult to control our emotions. However, you are reminded that if you wish to remain, you must be silent."

Kathleen saw a restraining hand grasp her father's shoulder and he sat down.

Chairman Paul turned to Kathleen. "Please answer my question."

"My answer is an emphatic <u>no</u>," she replied, through clenched teeth.

Chairman Paul looked at his colleagues. He asked, "Do you have any questions for this witness?"

Three heads shook in unison.

He said, "You're excused, Miss Matthews. Thank you for your contribution to our deliberations."

Kathleen left the room and went downstairs to wait for her father.

It took a few minutes to sort out her thoughts but, soon enough, it became clear that Chairman Paul was determined to find her complicit in some way. She wondered to what extent his son, Malcolm, helped him to formulate his questions. Did father and son share the same view of women in medicine, or in any profession for that matter?

She felt a hand on her shoulder, turned, and saw her father's angry expression.

Her anger erupted, "I'm a drug addict, a murderer, a trollop, a liar."

Her father said, "I understand your anger and I'm sorry Kathleen. Had I known the chairman would be so aggressive, I'd have looked for a way to spare you."

"It's not your fault, Daddy. I suspect he's had other influences on him. I don't know if I've told you this but his son, Malcolm, resents my being in the medical program. He's done everything he can to embarrass and humiliate me."

"You didn't tell me that, but it explains Richard Paul's approach. He bullied you and it sullied his reputation in my eyes, and, I hope, in the eyes of others."

Kathleen asked, "Now what?"

He replied, "The committee will make recommendations to Sir John and he'll decide what's to be done."

"How long will it take?"

"They won't meet on Saturday or Sunday, perhaps in a few days."

"Should I be worried?" Kathleen asked.

Chapter 48 Bad Habits

Ward 5

"Pssst…Billy! Got any food?"

Lundy was half way to sleep and it took a few seconds for the voice to register. His cell was almost dark with a faint glow on the wall opposite his small window.

"You awake?" the voice sounded again, from the cell opposite.

Lundy swung his legs over the side, and walked barefoot to the door. Spilled food and other detritus layered the splintered pine floor and stuck to the bottoms of his feet.

He felt better in recent days but his mind was occasionally foggy, especially late at night. However, he could now focus his thoughts and remember things. He didn't want the attendants, especially the skinny one, to find out that he had improved.

He opened his meal slot. "Ripper, what do you want?" he said, in a loud whisper.

"Name's Waldo, got any food, Billy?"

"I'm Ernie, not Billy. No food, Waldo. What time is it?"

"Dunno, can't see out, got no window."

"I got a window, it's night and quiet, that's all I can tell," Lundy replied.

"Must be after midnight," Ripper said.

"Can't you sleep?" Lundy asked.

"Nope, can't tell day from night. Sometimes I sleep all day, might as well be dead."

Lundy heard the rattle of keys and the screech of hinges.

Shouts came from the cells. "Yeeeaaaa!… Weasel!… Weasel!"

"Hush up, attendants coming," Lundy said.

He backed away from the door and crouched in the corner. Footsteps came closer, stopped every so often, and then they moved away. Lundy heard the door to the cell block open and close and he crept back.

Lundy said, "You been in long?"

Ripper replied, "Too long, can't remember."

Lundy asked, "Any way out?"

Ripper laughed, "Not much chance. I get out maybe once a week while they clean my cell. You gonna try?"

"Thinkin' about it," Lundy replied.

"Maybe I can help."

"How?"

"I know some things."

"What things?"

"Where they hang the keys, shift rotations, attendant's bad habits."

"Like what?"

"When Davies is on the midnight shift, he sneaks down to the kitchen to steal food and leaves Frost alone."

"That's interesting and I could use your help, but I'm not ready. Need more thinking, need a plan," Lundy said.

"When you're ready, let me know and I'll help."

"Thanks-"

A shout came from the far end of the hall, "Stop the yakking, don't make me come down."

Lundy whispered, "Later…"

Chapter 49 Well Done

Following her appearance before the committee, Kathleen felt angry.

It's not fair! I did nothing wrong.

She waited near the door of the lecture theatre and watched for Claire. She wanted her friend with her when she entered the classroom because, she was quite sure, Malcolm Paul knew about her Committee appearance and would look for ways to embarrass her. The students who passed by her seemed oblivious to her anxiety. Once or twice, she peeked into the classroom and saw Malcolm Paul, with his friends. She thought about entering the classroom alone, but then Claire appeared, bustling along, late as usual.

Kathleen opened the door. "Hurry on, Claire, we don't want to be late."

Claire replied, "Don't get your knickers in a knot, I'm coming."

They sat down just as Professor Lupei entered carrying the mid term test papers.

Claire leaned over and whispered, "Oh-oh, midterm results."

Professor Lupei set the test papers on the desk and said, "I'm generally pleased with the results of your mid term tests. Let me provide you with a summary of class results."

He walked to the blackboard and wrote:

Average class mark = 76.2
Highest class mark = 96.4
Lowest class mark = 52.6

He continued, "Your mark represents 30% of your final mark. If you scored below 60 you are at risk of failure."

He asked students to come forward to pick up their tests when he called their names. Kathleen felt confident and she watched the parade of students and studied their faces. When her name was called she stepped forward to retrieve her test paper. Professor Lupei held it just long enough to get her attention. She raised her head and looked at him. She was surprised to see a faint smile from a man who rarely smiled. He leaned forward and whispered, "Well done Miss Matthews."

She murmured, "Thank you."

Her eyes widened when she saw the mark, 96.4, the highest mark in the class. She floated back to her seat.

The highest mark, I can't believe it!

Claire said, "You look like the cat that ate a flock of canaries."

Kathleen revealed the mark on her test paper.

Claire poked her. "Good for you! That'll show 'em."

Kathleen's flushed appearance and the tête-à-tête between them did not go unnoticed on the other side of the room.

When the class ended Claire bounced out of her seat and Kathleen caught the sleeve of her jacket. "Let's stay behind for a minute, I want Malcolm Paul and his friends to leave first so I can avoid him."

Claire sat down and they shuffled papers until the classroom emptied. Kathleen emerged, looked left and right, and decided the coast was clear. There was no sign of Malcolm Paul and his friends. Kathleen parted company with Claire when they left the Medical Building. She felt good and walked briskly homeward.

She passed through the campus gates and heard a familiar voice behind her. "Enjoy it while you can," Malcolm Paul said.

Kathleen turned to face him. "I do enjoy it, very much," she said.

He narrowed his eyes which gave his thin face added menace. "I'm guessing your joy won't last very long."

She brought out her test paper, waved it, and said, "I assume you got a good mark on the midterm test."

"It wasn't the top mark but I'm satisfied with it. I'm aiming to win the gold medal," he replied. He took two giant strides towards her.

He's dying to know.

She stuffed the test paper into her case and turned away. She walked briskly but heard his feet pounding to catch up. He grabbed her by the shoulder. She stopped and twisted, and he lost his grip.

"Don't touch me!" she said.

He looked surprised, "I barely touched you."

She replied, "Don't touch me, barely or otherwise."

She aimed a barbed question at him. "What was your mark on the midterm?"

"None of your business."

"It wasn't as good as mine."

He looked confused and said, "How could you possibly know that."

"You're a smart man, you figure it out."

***

Chapter 50 Cell Talk

Ward 5

Ernie Lundy stirred and moaned. In his dream, his father's contorted face was inches away and the gold tooth flashed. Furious fists rose and fell and little Ernie fell to the floor. His ears rang. The toe of a boot collapsed his stomach and he couldn't breathe. He looked for his mother. She was on the other side of the room, splayed in a corner with blood oozing from her nose. Her cheap necklace was broken and dangling. She raised herself up, and shouted, "Stop… please stop… he's just a little boy… he didn't mean it."

She sounded whiny, it was a pitiful plea.

Lundy awoke in a cold sweat. "Never again, never again," he shouted. His fingers touched his chest, looking for his long lost talisman.

"You okay?" called Waldo Speight, from the cell opposite.

"Yeah, bad dream," said Lundy

"What time is it?" Speight asked.

"Still dark, after midnight. What's keeping you awake?"

"I ain't gonna last, I gotta get out of here," said Speight.

Lundy said, "Me too, I - "

A voice shouted from the attendants lunchroom, "Shut up down there…"

Lundy lowered his voice, "Escape, is what I'm thinking, you with me?"

"All I think about. Can't do it alone though."

"We need a plan."

Speight whispered, "Think you're up to it?"

"What do you mean?"

"You been some kinda boob for months, how come you're so smart all of a sudden?"

"Can't explain it. Woke up one morning and my brain started working. I remembered things."

"You still sound dumb sometimes. Does your brain stop and start, just like that?"

"No, my brain's working fine, I play dumb so they don't suspect."

Speight said, "You're stupid-smart. I got some ideas about escape but we have to work together on it. One guy can't do it."

"What do you –"

The door to the cellblock groaned open and heavy boots thudded down the hall. Lundy closed the slot, retreated to his bed, and waited. He heard heavy breathing and light from a hurricane lantern seeped around his door. The footsteps retreated and the door to the cellblock clanged shut.

Lundy opened his slot and whispered, "You still there?"

Speight replied, "Still here, wide awake."

"What's our plan?"

"I have some ideas."

"Let's hear 'em."

"We're in this together, you agree?"

"I agree, now tell me."

"It's got to be on the midnight shift with Frost and Davies."

"Why then, why them?"

"Davies has a sweet tooth, he's got a key to the kitchen, just before morning shift change, he sneaks downstairs and grabs some sweets. I hear them laughing and carrying on when he comes back."

"What's the plan?"

"He's absent for maybe 20 minutes so there's only Frost. Frost has a short fuse, we can play on that."

"What do we do?"

"I haven't figured it out but, somehow, we lure Frost into a cell, overpower him, take his keys, and escape."

"They never come into a cell alone, always in pairs, it's a rule. I don't think it'll work."

"You got a better plan?"

Lundy raised his voice. "Don't get shirty. Can we make your plan work?"

"Pipe down, or we'll be licked before we start."

Lundy thought for a moment and then said, "Whose cell do we lure him into?"

"I'm thinking, yours."

"Why me? Frost hates my guts."

"Exactly why it needs to be your cell."

"What are you doing while Frost is kicking the shit out of me?"

"I'm raising hell, screaming, maybe something like, 'he's hung himself' or, 'he's escaped', anything to get his attention and bring him down here."

"Then what?"

"I rile up the other inmates. They make a hell of a racket and I keep yelling at Frost. I've seen it before, Frost gets all wound up and just has to beat on somebody."

"He's done it? He's gone into a cell alone?"

"Yeah, once or twice. He got away with it, nothing happened."

The door to the cellblock clanged open and the attendant yelled, "One more sound and I'm going to beat the living daylights out of somebody. Now shut up!"

He banged his club on the bars.

Speight whispered, "We'll talk later."

★ ★ ★

Chapter 51 Not Good News

"I'm afraid it's not good news," her father said.

Kathleen bit her lip, closed the door and followed her father into her living room. He sat in the armchair by the window and she sat on the sofa and curled her legs beneath her. She knew he was studying her face, assessing her.

She wasn't ready to talk and looked past him, through the window. The gas lamps cast shadows on the building opposite.

Not good news? What now?

She slowly exhaled, raised her head, and cleared her throat. "Tell me," she said.

He replied, "It may not be as bad as you think."

"What is it?"

"There was a meeting of the board late this afternoon to consider the recommendations of the Disciplinary Committee."

Kathleen bit her lip. "What happened?"

"That's just it, I don't know. Before the meeting began, Sir John took me aside and suggested I not attend."

"Because of me?"

"Yes, Sir John told me your name would come up."

"Does it mean I should expect punishment?"

"Not necessarily, he just said your name would come up. Don't read too much into it."

"It can't be good."

"We'll have to wait and see how it turns out. I don't like the way your situation was handled and I told him so."

"I hope you kept your temper."

TJ gave a wry smile. "I didn't punch him in the nose, although I felt like it."

Kathleen walked to the window. The street below was almost deserted and a bell for evening mass sounded in the distance. She said, "I can't imagine why they would want to penalize me."

"Nor can I," her father replied.

"When will I know?"

"Jim Scott is on the committee, he's a good friend of mine. I'll speak with him and find out what's going on."

Kathleen turned away from the window. "I'm beginning to regret my decision to study medicine."

"Don't say that. I know it's discouraging but things will get better, you'll see."

"I hope you're right."

He said, "I have to go. I'll call Jim Scott in the morning."

They walked to the door and he said, "Regardless of how this turns out, I'm considering resigning from the Board. I just don't like the way they've gone about this."

She said, "I know you're upset. I don't want you to resign on my account, please stay on, at least until we know the outcome."

He replied, "I won't do anything until we know."

Kathleen watched her father walk down the hall. He was slightly stooped and walked slowly. He wasn't yet an old man but the signs were there. She sighed and closed the door.

***

That evening, Kathleen replayed their conversation over and over.

Stop worrying.

She remembered tomorrow's German test and took out her textbook. She was well prepared but decided to study anyway if for no other reason than to take her mind off things. She placed a pillow against the upholstered arm of the sofa, tucked in her legs, and sat with the book in her lap.

She awoke with a start when the phone rang and her German book hit the floor with a loud thud.

What time is it?

She stumbled into the hall and glanced at the clock in the kitchen.

9:30 PM, I've been asleep for an hour.

"Hello…"

He said, "I almost hung up. Is it a bad time?"

It took a few seconds to recognize the voice.

Not you!

She replied, "It's always a bad time where you're concerned, Mr Moyer. It's late and I'm tired."

"I wouldn't have called if I didn't think it was important."

"Important to you or to me?"

"Both of us."

"I'm not in a mood to talk."

"I have the Disciplinary Committee report."

"I don't believe you."

"I'm looking at it as we speak. I'll read a section…"

He read and the more he read the more authentic it seemed.

He said, "Heard enough? Are you convinced?"

I ought to hang up, but I've got to find out.

"How did you get it? The report is supposed to be confidential."

Bad Medicine

"It arrived at the Gazette in a brown envelope with my name on it. I don't know who sent it but it looks real enough to me."

"What if it's not? What if it's a fake and someone sent it to you, to embarrass you and the Gazette."

"I've already talked to someone who knows what the report contains. I'm convinced it's real."

"A spy?"

"A source."

"I understand why this report is important to you, but why is it important to me?"

"Because you're mentioned in it, that's why. I thought you'd like to know what it says."

She thought of saying she didn't care but, of course, she knew she did. She found some pleasure in imagining his disappointment. However, like the proverbial cat, her curiosity got the better of her.

"What does the report say?"

"Are you sitting down?"

"Get on with it, Mr Moyer."

"Let me see…"

She heard paper rustling in the background. He continued, "Page 11, recommendations…"

She covered the mouthpiece and took a deep breath. He read, "Miss Matthews could be considered an innocent party. However, she knew about Professor Ducharme's drug use and deliberately decided not to tell anyone. Had she done so, she might have saved the university a great deal of embarrassment. Whether or not Miss Matthews was motivated by a clandestine affair with Dr Ducharme, a married man, the Committee has insufficient evidence to reach a conclusion."

An affair!

"It's completely unfair!" Kathleen exclaimed.

"Those are not my words, Miss Matthews, don't blame me."

Kathleen excused herself and dropped the earpiece. Her throat felt constricted and she went to the kitchen to get a drink of water. She felt like this once before, when she was bound and gagged on the dirt floor of the cabin, waiting for Lundy to return and finish her off.

She returned to the telephone and said, "I'm back. I believe you were going to read the Committee's recommendation."

"Are you ready?"

She took a deep breath and said, "Ready."

He read, "On a majority vote, the committee recommends Miss Matthews be placed on Student Probation for the balance of the academic year."

She dropped the earpiece and sank to the floor with her back to the wall. Moyer's voice, faint and garbled, droned nearby.

Probation!

A tinny voice sounded, "Are you there?... Miss Matthews, are you there?"

She got to her feet. "I'm sorry Mr Moyer, I lost the connection. It seems all right now, please continue."

He asked, "Where should I begin?"

"I heard about probation, perhaps you could continue after that."

"Let me see..."

Kathleen heard pages turning. "Probation...with the condition her academic and personal conduct is satisfactory. Her faculty supervisor, Professor Merrick, will submit a monthly report to the Dean of Students. Any breach of probation will result in expulsion."

She covered the mouthpiece and took deep breaths.

Expulsion!

For the first time in their conversation, she felt anger.

He said, "That's it, Miss Matthews. What's your reaction?"

She replied, "I don't know what to say, I just don't."

She heard the worst and, having heard it, her fear dissipated. Her mind cleared and she thought about the recommendation.

She said, "It's only a recommendation and Sir John makes the final decision."

He replied, "Yes, I believe that's true."

"Please read the first part again."

"On a majority vote the committee…"

"Stop right there!"Kathleen exclaimed.

"What's wrong?"

"Nothing's wrong. The committee's recommendation isn't unanimous, there was disagreement."

He said, "I don't see the significance."

"We'll see what Sir John decides."

"I'd like to have something for my story."

"I can't, I've got a lot to think about."

"We won't publish anything until we hear something official. I'll call you at that time to see if you have anything to say."

"I make no promises Mr Moyer. Now, if you excuse me, it's late, I have an exam tomorrow, and I must get to bed."

She hung up and thought about calling her father but it was late and she was tired.

Chapter 52 Recommendations

Kathleen woke early and thought about the Committee's recommendation.

Bad Medicine

It's been my misfortune to share classes with Richard Paul's son. He's spread the rumour I had an affair with Professor Ducharme.

She imagined Malcolm Paul gloating and holding the Gold Medal and she felt angry. She went into the kitchen for breakfast. Afterwards, she brushed up on her German verb tenses.

The phone rang.

"I'm glad I caught you before your class," her father said.

"I have a German test this morning," she replied.

"I won't keep you. I'm going to meet Jim Scott. I spoke with him yesterday and he agreed to tell me where things stood with respect to the Committee Report. Will you be home after lunch?"

"Yes, I'll be home all afternoon."

"I'll call you after my meeting."

She said, "There's something I need to tell you."

"What's that?"

"That Gazette reporter called me last night."

"Is he still bothering you? What did he want this time?"

"He obtained a copy of the Committee Report."

TJ guffawed, "I don't believe it."

"I didn't at first, but I'm convinced he's got it."

"How did he get it? Who gave it to him?"

"He said…a brown envelope. He said he has a source on the inside."

Kathleen described her conversation with Jimmy Moyer. When she finished, her father said, "I can't believe the Committee recommended probation with possible expulsion."

"I know, it's unbelievable, but the recommendation wasn't unanimous."

"If it wasn't unanimous, there's some hope. It might be Jim Scott who's objecting. It's good information to have for my meeting."

She asked, "Do you think Mr Scott will help?"

"I'm sure he'll do what he can. He's a good friend and he was influential in getting you into medicine."

She said, "I have to leave for class. Promise to call me this afternoon after your meeting."

"Yes, I will. Good luck with your test."

★★★

The German test was easy and Kathleen felt confident. She hurried home and just as she reached the landing, she heard her telephone. She hurried down the hall and opened the door.

"Hello," she said, and dropped her books at her feet.

"You sound out of breath," said her father.

"I just got here; give me a minute while I take off my coat."

She tossed her coat on the sofa and returned to the telephone. "Did you have your meeting with Mr Scott?"

"Yes, and he agreed to help."

"What will he do?"

"He objected to the committee's recommendation and he spoke to Sir John. He thinks it will have some effect."

"Some effect? What does that mean?"

"Punishing you on such flimsy grounds will damage McGill's reputation. He argued that there is growing political support for women in medicine and women will soon get the vote."

"You know Sir John better than I do, would he support that argument?"

"Sir John is set in his ways, but he's an intelligent man and Jim Scott is a very influential board member. It's hard to predict what Sir John will do but we'll cross that bridge when, and if, we come to it."

"What else did Mr Scott say?" she asked.

"The committee recommended Professor Harcourt's removal as Dean of Medicine."

"It's a surprise, at least to me. I wonder who will replace him."

"Professor Merrick, I'm told."

"An excellent choice."

"It's been difficult for you, Kathleen. How are you feeling?"

"I was down in the dumps for a while but now I'm angry. I don't know if Malcolm Paul influenced his father and I hate to think that's the way the world works."

"Is he the young man who's been giving you and Claire a difficult time?"

"Yes. His father attended McGill and received the gold medal for law. Malcolm wants to win the gold medal for medicine. He sees me as competition. Since I'm a woman, it fuels his ambition. I received the highest mark in our human anatomy midterm. His behaviour, and that of his friends, seems so petty, so unnecessary."

Her father sighed. "It may seem unnecessary, but, in my experience, it's the way people are. I see it in business every day. Some men want to win at any cost and heaven help anyone who gets in the way. Don't underestimate what Malcolm Paul will do to win."

"How could his father, a prominent lawyer, be so petty?"

"I don't know Richard Paul. His reputation is a win-at-any-cost lawyer. A great person to have on your side but a dangerous opponent."

Kathleen said, "We have to fight this."

"I agree, and we will. Any suggestions?"

"How many board members would support you?"

"I don't know. I'd like to think if Board members knew the facts many of them would side with Jim Scott, and support us."

"How can you find out?"

"I could discuss the situation with each board member. However, I must admit, I'm uncomfortable with lobbying board members on behalf of my family. It seems self-serving."

Kathleen said, "You can't let that get in the way. You're as important as anyone else on the board, and there's nothing wrong with advocating a just and sensible approach. It's anything but self-serving."

"Maybe you're right."

"I know I'm right."

Chapter 53 Out

Ward 5

"Psssst…you there?" the Ripper asked.

Lundy scrambled to his feet. "I'm here…you ready?"

Ripper said, "Frost and Davies just came on shift. They'll play cribbage for a couple of hours, eat lunch then doze. Before shift change, Davies will sneak off to the kitchen. That's when we do it."

Lundy asked, "Think you can sleep?"

"Maybe, don't worry, I'll be awake when the time comes. You go to sleep if you want to."

"Not sure I can, but I'll try."

Lundy lay on his bed and poked his hand through the hole in his mattress. He pulled out several bed spring attachments. He poked the hooks through the corners of his blanket and spread the blanket on the floor.

He lay on his bed and dozed off. He woke up with a start and listened. There wasn't a sound and, for a few seconds, he thought he had overslept. A burst of laughter came from the lunch room. The cribbage game was under way and he breathed a sigh of relief.

Twice during the next three hours, either Davies or Frost made a quick loop up and down the cellblock. Lundy traced their movements by the flicker of the hurricane lantern and the smell of kerosene. He sat on the floor with his back to the door and listened. He heard Ripper shuffling, across the hall. An hour passed and the sound of snoring from the lunch room meant the time was getting close.

The hinge on Ripper's' door creaked open and Ripper said, "Ernie, getting close, better get started."

Lundy replied, "Will do. I hope I can do this without making a sound."

Ripper said, "If you make a noise, we'll spend the rest of our lives in this dump."

Lundy replied, "Don't worry, I'll be quiet."

Lundy stripped his bed and dragged the bed frame to the door. He leaned one end of the frame against the wall. He shoved bedspring attachments in a crack in the floor so the frame wouldn't slip. He climbed this makeshift ladder with his blanket under his arm. He jammed bedspring attachments into the ceiling. He hung the blanket high above the door, and slipped behind it. It was near perfect. He was invisible to anyone entering the room, especially in the dark.

He climbed down, opened the meal slot, and whispered, "All set."

He sat on the floor with his back to the door and listened. Time passed slowly and then he heard chairs scraping on hardwood, muffled voices, and the rattling of keys.

Ripper said, "Davies is gone, take your position. When Frost appears, I'll start yelling. Hide so Frost doesn't see you."

Lundy climbed the makeshift ladder and hid. The channel of the door frame was an uncomfortable place to stand. When he settled behind the blanket, he kicked the bed frame and it hit the floor with a clatter. Lundy held fast and his feet, perched on the door channel, hurt like hell.

Ripper screamed. "He's done it! Suicide! Help! Help!"

Frost yelled, "What's going on down there?"

Keys rattled and boots pounded down the hall.

Ripper yelled, "He's done it! Suicide! Help him."

Frost arrived, breathless, and said, "Who? Help who?"

"Billy Boo Boo, the dumb shit! He's killed himself!"

Lundy's door opened and light from the hurricane lantern illuminated his cell.

Frost said, "It's hard to see, the bed is tipped over but I don't see him."

Ripper said, "You have to help."

Ripper's plea was picked up by the other inmates and soon the cell block was a riot of noise and confusion.

Frost yelled, "Lundy, where are you? Show yourself."

Lundy sensed panic in Frost's voice. Frost stood in the doorway but did not enter.

Lundy's feet hurt and his calf muscles ached.

Come in, you skinny bastard.

Ripper yelled, "Frost, you can't just stand there. He's dying, do something!"

Frost yelled, "Shut up Speight! Shut your fat face! I'm trying to think."

Ripper shouted, "While you're standing in the doorway with your finger up your ass, Billy's bleeding to death on the floor. Do something!"

Lundy heard a club clang against the door and Frost screamed, "Ripper, don't make me come after you!"

Ripper replied, "Clubbing me won't help Billy. Do something. Do something smart, for once in your life."

A chorus of inmate voices chanted, "Do something… Weasel… do something…"

Lundy's legs cramped and he wasn't sure how much longer he could hold out. He heard Frost enter his cell and light haloed the edge of the blanket.

Frost kicked at the upturned bed, and walked around the cell. He yelled,"he ain't here! The bugger's gone!"

Lundy peeked out and saw Frost with his back to him. He jumped, and landed on Frost's back driving him, face first, into the floor. Frost's lantern shattered and a river of flame streaked towards the upturned mattress.

Ripper yelled, "The keys! Get his keys!"

Lundy tore the key ring from Frost's outstretched hand. Frost tried to get up and Lundy delivered two hard kicks to Frost's ribs, driving him, face first, into the floor. Frost gulped for breath and rolled onto his back.

Lundy left the cell and locked the door. Frost had his legs drawn up and moaned like a sick dog. The mattress burned.

Ripper yelled, "Over here, bring the keys, let me out."

Lundy looked down the hall to the wide open door at the end of the cellblock. His thoughts were interrupted when Ripper yelled, "Get me out!"

Lundy unlocked Ripper's door and they ran down the hall and inmates screamed to be set free.

"Don't stop," said the Ripper.

They reached the end of the hall and Lundy saw smoke billow from his cell.

Ripper nudged him. "Hurry up, Davies will be back any minute."

Chapter 54 Run For It

They stood at the top of the stairwell and looked down.

"Seems quiet," Lundy said.

Ripper replied, "It won't be for long, let's get outta here."

They double stepped to the bottom of the stairs.

Lundy said, "I remember, this leads to reception and the street. One mad dash and we're free. Ripper replied, "One step at a time, open the door, try one of those keys."

Lundy checked the key ring and tried several keys before he found the right one. He cracked the door and peered into the hall. "I see a couple of attendants."

Ripper said, "Must be shift change, better get a move on."

Lundy peeked through the door and saw an attendant talking with a nurse. He quickly closed the door and said, "It's Davies, he's out there."

Ripper gripped Lundy's arm. "Can he see us?"

Lundy opened the door. "No, he's got his back to the door."

Ripper pushed Lundy. "Move! Move!"

Lundy kept his eye on Davies as he crossed the hall. He looked longingly at the main doors and beyond, to the street, freedom.

Ripper grabbed his arm. "Over here," he said and pulled Lundy into an alcove.

Lundy said, "Let's make a run for it."

Ripper replied, "No, the longer it takes to discover we're missing, the better our chances. Let's go before someone spots us."

They moved in single file with their backs to the wall. Ripper said, "Try the doors. We need a place to catch our breath and think."

A door opened and they froze. An attendant emerged, three doors down. Lundy held his breath. The attendant turned right and disappeared through a door, further down the hall.

"Let's go into the room he came out of," Ripper said.

A single light bulb burned brightly in what looked like a changing room. Attendant uniforms lay on shelves and street clothes hung on hooks.

Ripper pointed to the uniforms. "What do you think?"

"What about civvies?" Lundy replied, and tried on a coat. It was far too small for his large frame. "Maybe not," he said.

Ripper pulled at his dirty grey shirt, "We can't walk around like this."

They put on attendants' uniforms, white pants and blue jackets. Lundy liked the sharp crease in the pants but his inmate shoes were scruffy.

"Our shoes will be a dead giveaway," he said.

"Nobody looks at shoes," Ripper replied.

"Women do," Lundy said.

Ripper made a face and shrugged.

"What now?" Lundy asked.

"Do we stick together or split up?"

"What difference does it make?"

"A big difference. If we stick together, it's easier to spot us. They'll be looking for two men with our descriptions. The odds are better if we split up."

"We could stick together now and split up later."

"No, we'd better do it now. Once Davies gets back, he'll sound the alarm and this place will be crawling with cops."

"Okay. Who goes first?"

"I'll go," Ripper said. He turned to Lundy and said, "Remember, you're an attendant not an inmate, so act like one."

Ripper nodded and slipped out the door.

Lundy waited and listened. All was quiet outside and, it seemed, Ripper got away. Lundy stepped out, squared his shoulders, and walked to the end of the corridor. He opened a door and faced a stairwell. He closed the door and listened for footsteps on the stairs. Hearing nothing, he walked to the bottom. He figured he was in the basement because the floors were concrete, and it had a dank root cellar smell.

A dim bulb dangled from the ceiling near another door. He walked to the door and gripped the handle. He heard a noise, turned, and saw a gurney banging through a doorway several doors down. He took two quick steps and found himself in a large room with a high ceiling, perhaps twelve feet or more. In the dim light he made out several tables lined up on either side. The sounds in the corridor grew louder and he hid beneath a table. Something struck his face and he brushed it aside. It swung back and struck again. It felt cold, rigid and oddly familiar.

A dead man's hand! I'm in the morgue!

He shuddered and scrunched down.

The door latch clicked and a shaft of light swept across the floor and a gurney banged through the door. A light switch snapped and he peeked out. The gurney wheeled towards him and he slipped beneath another table. He peeked out and saw a garage door at the far end of the room.

My escape route.

He raised his head and saw the attendant shift a body from the gurney to a table. The attendant wheeled the gurney to the door, turned out the light and left.

Now what, how do I get out of here?

He listened for signs that the escape had been discovered. All was quiet, so far, so good. He crept towards the garage door but stopped when an adjacent door opened and two attendants walked into the room. One of the attendants grabbed a chain, and, with some difficulty, he opened the garage door.

He said, "I thought they were going to grease the pulleys. This gets harder every time."

It took a few seconds for Lundy's eyes to adjust to the intrusion of light. A vehicle backed down the sloped driveway. It was black with **Ambulance** stencilled in white across the rear doors. He crawled closer and watched the men load two bodies into the ambulance.

One of them said, "I'm going to grab a quick coffee, I need something to pick me up before we deliver those stiffs."

"I'll go with you, I could use a coffee," his partner said.

"Get the garage door."

"Will do…go ahead, I'll catch up."

The door came down a lot easier than it went up and the attendants left the room. Lundy tried the entry door but it was locked. He tried the keys on Frost's ring without success and then tried to raise the garage door but he couldn't muster the strength.

I'm not half the man I used to be.

Things seemed quiet, at least for now, but the alarm would soon be raised and all hell would break loose. Time was slipping away and escape via the morgue seemed like his best opportunity. He opened a back door of the ambulance and jumped inside. He crouched between the two bodies, one on either side.

Where to hide?

He felt around for a weapon but found nothing. He closed the doors and crouched down, ready to spring.

The sickly sweet smell of death made him gag. Voices grew louder. He tensed when the garage door opened. The engine coughed, caught, revved, and the ambulance jerked forward. It chugged up an incline and picked up speed.

He considered escape plans, including a jump out the rear door. He decided he would hide by replacing one of the dead bodies, since it was unlikely anyone would suspect a dead body and, no matter where this journey ended, he'd still have an opportunity to escape. Meanwhile, he needed to put as much distance as possible between himself and the Institute.

He rolled a body onto the floor and stripped the identifying tag from its big toe. He opened the door, scanned the street, shoved the body and watched it bounce, tumble, and roll. He found it amusing to think of the body being discovered and people wondering how it got there.

He removed his shoes and socks, tucked them under the sheet, rolled up his pant legs, and attached the toe tag.

Thanks for the tag, Alfie Goodick.

* * *

Chapter 55 Dead Man

Lundy lay on the stretcher, like a dead man, with a toe tag on his exposed foot.

What happened to Ripper?

Except for a faint halo of light around the ambulance doors, it was pitch black. He changed his mind about making a run for it. His new plan was to stay put and find an opportunity to get away. His thoughts were interrupted by a change in pitch of the engine and a noticeable slowing down. The ride was surprisingly brief, probably less than ten minutes. He worried about being so close to the Institute where a search might already be underway.

The ambulance stopped, turned, and backed up. The passenger side door opened and closed. He pulled the sheet over his face and tucked his arms by his side. He managed his breathing lest the rise and fall of the sheet give him away. The engine idled and he heard the clank and grind of a large door. The ambulance backed up and, seconds later, it stopped. The driver cut the engine and, for a few seconds, all was quiet. He heard footsteps outside the door of the ambulance and he tensed. Someone clambered into the back and he heard a stretcher slide across the floor. "Hold on, give me a chance to get my feet under me," one of the attendants said.

"All set?" said the other

"All set, let's go," came the reply.

He heard them huff and strain and carry their burden. When they left, he peeked through the rear door and saw a large room. It had benches, sinks, and shelves full of glassware. It looked like a laboratory. A man in a white coat had his back to him. The man was of average height with a full head of hair, mostly black with some grey. He couldn't understand what was said but the man directed the attendants. Lundy expected the attendants to return and he pulled the sheet over him. Moments later he was carried into the room and laid on a table. No one looked under the sheet, it was quiet, and he felt safe, for now.

I pulled it off.

The ambulance and attendants left but he wasn't sure about the man in the white coat. He lifted the sheet and looked around. He was alone. He stripped away the sheet and slid off the table. He sat down, removed the toe tag and put on his socks and shoes. There were several tables in the room, one of which contained the body of his ambulance companion. He examined the garage door and was disappointed to find a padlock on the chain hoist. The door next to it was also locked. He looked through the window and saw well manicured lawns, shrubbery, and what looked like an entrance to the building he occupied. A young man, who looked like a student, came around the corner and entered the building. He searched the room for tools, clothing, or any device that might facilitate his escape. A change of clothing would be ideal but, aside from long white coats and rubber aprons, there was nothing suitable.

He saw a set of double doors at the far end of the room. He hurried over, opened a door and stepped into a long corridor. A sign on the wall told him the room he left was the Cadaver Lab. He hoped the corridor might be escape route and he began a cautious exploration. A door opened further down the hall and he heard voices. He retreated back into the Cadaver Lab, ran across the room and hid in a storage room near the alcove. He nudged the door open and watched. The doors to the room swung open and the man in the white coat returned.

Chapter 56 Alfie

Kathleen's Apartment

Kathleen woke before dawn and thought about the events of the past few days.

What will happen?

She washed and dressed and made tea and toast. She took her breakfast into the living room, sat on the sofa, and reviewed her anatomy notes. She was surprised by the marginal note on today's schedule. It was her turn to assist Mike Avila in the Cadaver Lab and she had to be there by 8:30 AM. She gave an exaggerated sigh when she saw that Malcolm Paul would be her lab partner.

I'm in no mood for any of his snide remarks.

She arrived at the classroom at 8:25 AM and placed her books on her desk. Malcolm waited near the exit door. He looked impatient. He held the door and made a 'hurry up' gesture. She was tight-lipped as she approached the door.

"After you Dr Matthews," he said, and laughed.

She said, "Thank you, Nurse Paul," and breezed past him.

He caught up to her. "I don't like this any more than you do."

She replied, "Our work in the lab counts toward our class mark so let's do a good job. "

He said, "Why didn't you take up nursing?"

"It's the 20th century, or hadn't you noticed. The world is changing and I'm nobody's handmaiden."

They continued in frosty silence into the Cadaver Lab.

Avila said, "We've got a lot of work to do, so let's get started. Mr Paul, I'd like you to prepare Ebenezer for today's class. I'll help you lift him onto a table. I want you to give his spinal column a close inspection and an application of Formalin. I know you've used Formalin before but I want to emphasize its hazards, so be careful."

He turned to Kathleen. "Miss Matthews, we've just received two cadavers from the Institute and I'd like you to assist me with the paperwork. I'll join you after I've helped Malcolm."

Kathleen asked, "Where are they?"

Avila pointed towards the garage doors. "In the alcove, by the storage room, two tables, they're covered with white sheets."

Avila passed a sheaf of papers to Kathleen and joined Malcolm at the holding tank.

Kathleen found a pencil and walked to the alcove. She found one of the bodies but not the second one. A crumpled white sheet lay on the floor, next to an empty table.

He said there were two cadavers.

She checked the information sheets and matched the name on the toe tag with the name on one of the sheets but she couldn't find the second cadaver, Alfie Goodick, male, age forty-six.

She walked back to Avila. "Mr Avila, I found one of the cadavers, but I couldn't find the second one. Could he be somewhere else?"

Avila looked at her with a puzzled expression. "You're sure? You looked everywhere?"

Malcolm guffawed, "Elementary physiology, Miss Matthews, dead men can't walk."

Kathleen ignored the remark and showed the information sheet to Avila. "I couldn't find this one, Goodick."

Avila looked at Malcolm and said, "I hope this isn't another student prank."

Malcolm raised his palms and shrugged.

"Let's have a look," Avila said, and beckoned to Kathleen. "Come with me."

Chapter 57 Footsteps

Lundy

Lundy heard approaching footsteps and quietly eased open the storage room door. Someone came into view, a woman. His eyes widened. It, was…her, Kathleen Matthews.

What's she doing here? Where am I anyway?

He watched her examine the cadaver and check the toe tag. The cotton sheet that once covered him lay crumpled on the floor. She picked it up, folded it, and placed it on the table. She studied a sheet of paper, shook her head, and left.

He followed the sound of her footsteps and she spoke with someone, a man. He couldn't make out her side of the conversation, but he heard the man say, "Let's have a look."

Then, footsteps, headed his way. He closed the door and tried to collect his thoughts.

Make a run for it? Stay here? I need a weapon.

His eyes adjusted to the darkness and he explored his hiding place. Shelves lined both sides of the narrow room. It was too dark to see clearly and he ran his hand along the shelves to his left. There were bottles, boxes and glass containers but nothing he might use as a weapon. On the other side, on the bottom shelf, he felt something metallic. He felt the sharp, toothy, edge of a saw with a cold metal handle, a weapon.

***

Kathleen

Kathleen said, "This table is empty."

She picked up the folded sheet. "Here's the shroud but there's no Alfie Goodick."

She looked behind her. "The other cadaver is over there, where they left him."

Avila shook his head. "It's a prank. I saw two cadavers, and I checked them both before I left. Somebody moved Goodick, and I think I know who."

He yelled, "Mr Paul, come here please."

Seconds later, and slightly out of breath, Malcolm stood before Avila. "Yes, Mr Avila."

Avila displayed a wry smile and said, "As the parrot said to the magician, what did you do with the body?"

Malcolm swallowed hard and managed to say, "I don't know."

"You're a prankster, Mr Paul, but this has ceased to be funny."

Avila advanced and Malcolm retreated until he bumped against the storage room door.

Avila asked, "What did you do with Alfie Goodick?"

Malcolm stammered, "I… I… don't know… anything, I swear."

Avila looked at Kathleen. "This is very serious, I'll have to report this to Professor Lupei. "Suddenly, the storage room door cracked open and a white-sleeved arm encircled Malcolm's neck.

Malcolm made an animal-like sound.

A few seconds passed before Kathleen registered the scene before her.

Lundy held Malcolm in the crook of his arm and pressed the edge of the bone saw to Malcolm's throat.

He said to Avila, "You're going to get me out of here or I'll cut this man's head off." He grabbed a fistful of Malcolm's hair, pulled his head back, and exposed his neck. He poked Malcolm's neck with the sharp point of the blade and Malcolm yelped.

Lundy will kill him!

Lundy shouted to Avila, "Hey! Mr White Coat! I want your clothes and I want the door open!"

Avila stepped forward. "Let him go."

Lundy jerked Malcolm's head and snarled, "Back off! I'm in charge here."

Avila didn't move and Lundy nicked Malcolm's chin with the sharp point of the blade. Malcolm howled and a rivulet of blood trickled down his neck onto his white collar.

Avila retreated further.

Kathleen stepped between Lundy and Avila and said, "You remember me, don't you?"

Lundy laughed and looked at her, as though she just said the dumbest thing anyone had ever said. "How could I forget you, Miss Matthews? We spent so many delightful moments together in days gone by."

Keep him talking.

"If you let Malcolm go, I promise I'll open the door and you can escape."

Lundy smirked, "I'm not stupid. What do you take me for? My days of pain and confusion are over.

Never again. I'm getting out of here and I'll do whatever I have to, that includes cutting the throat of this blubbering idiot."

Lundy shook Malcolm like a rag doll. "Stop snivelling!"

Avila moved and Lundy sliced the air with a cutting gesture.

Kathleen looked at Avila. "I know this man Mr Avila, he's capable of anything. Let's do what he says."

Avila looked confused. Lundy laughed and nicked Malcolm's chin again.

Lundy pointed his weapon at Avila, and said, "I want your clothes Mr White Coat, take 'em off."

Avila hesitated and Lundy said, "Now!"

Avila looked at Kathleen and gestured with embarrassment. She looked away.

Lundy pointed his weapon at Kathleen. "Bring those clothes here."

Kathleen turned her back to Lundy. Avila looked helpless, naked, except for his underwear, shoes and socks. She gave him a reassuring smile and saw Avila's eyes look down and to his right. He repeated the gesture.

She bent down and picked up Avila's apron. Lundy shouted at her, "I don't need that, put it down."

She held the apron close to her body and reached into the front pocket and felt the handle of a scalpel. She slid the scalpel under the sleeve of her blouse.

"Hurry up, bring me the shirt and pants," Lundy said.

She picked up the shirt and pants and turned to face Lundy.

"Come closer and hold them where I can see them."

Kathleen held the shirt and pants and stood in front of Lundy.

"Put them on the floor."

When she bent down, Lundy grabbed a handful of her hair and jerked her upward. She cried out in pain.

Avila stepped forward and Lundy threatened. "Stay where you are or I'll cut his throat and then hers."

Avila backed away.

Kathleen's head twisted around and Lundy put his cheek next to hers. His foul breath sickened her, and she remembered her painful experience at the Quarry. This time she didn't feel fear, she felt anger and a fierce determination to survive.

The door opened at the far end of the lab and Fatso's voice rang out, "Anybody here?"

What's he doing here!

Lundy tightened his grip on her hair and whispered, "Be quiet or else."

Kathleen heard Fatso's plodding footsteps and wished he would turn around and leave.

Fatso stood in the alcove with his mouth open. He looked at Lundy and said, "What are you doing?"

What do you think he's doing?

Lundy laughed and said, "You see that chair over there, fat boy? Drop your fat ass down and don't make a move or you'll be ankle-deep in your own blood."

Fatso jerked as though he had stuck his finger in a light socket. He ran to the nearest chair, sat down with his face frozen in a wide eyed stare.

Lundy loosened his grip on Kathleen's hair. "Help me get these clothes on."

"You'll have to take your jacket and shirt off and free up your arms."

She felt the scalpel move in her cuff and she held it in place with her pinky finger. "Undo the buttons," he said.

Malcolm whimpered and Lundy rapped his head with the butt of the saw.

It took several awkward contortions before Kathleen managed to get Avila's shirt on Lundy without dropping the scalpel.

"Now the pants," he said.

He wound her hair tightly as she undid his belt and eased down his pants. The stench of body odour and stale urine was overpowering.

Lundy bent his leg. "One leg at a time."

Kathleen bent as far as she could and his grip on her hair tightened. Her scalp felt numb. She tugged his pants down, but couldn't get his pants leg over his shoe.

"I'll have to take your shoe off," she said.

Lundy raised his foot and poked her in the ribs. "Dammit all, it ain't that complicated."

She snapped, "See for yourself."

"OK…take the damned shoe off."

Fatso piped up, "Maybe I can help."

Lundy shouted at him. "Shut your fat face!"

Fatso's head snapped around and he looked at the floor.

Lundy balanced on one leg while Kathleen tugged his pants leg over his shoe.

She worked her fingers and the scalpel slid into her hand.

She jerked Lundy's leg upward and he fell backward. He lost his grip on her hair and Malcolm fell forward. She felt blood on her face and tasted its saltiness. She saw Malcolm on the floor with a blood-stained face.

Lundy's weapon was on the floor and she saw him crawl towards it. She lunged, and knocked the saw across the room. Lundy pounced and grabbed her by the throat. He dug his thumbs into her larynx. The pain was excruciating and she couldn't breathe. In a desperate move, she rammed the scalpel into his throat. She was blinded by the blood that sprayed in heartbeat pulses.

His grip loosened and he fell forward. She wiped blood from her eyes and wiggled free of a twitching Lundy. Lundy writhed and rolled onto his back clawing at the handle of the scalpel buried deep in his throat.

Fatso danced up and down like a loose-stringed puppet. He yelled, "Oh my God! Oh my God!"

Kathleen sat on her heels with her head bowed. Avila rushed to her side and put his arm around her.

"You're bleeding, lie down, let me help you."

She lifted her head and saw Malcolm trying to get up.

She grabbed Avila's hand and said, "You'd better tend to Malcolm."

"You're sure you're not hurt?" Avila asked.

"I'm not badly hurt. Malcolm needs help."

Avila fashioned a crude bandage from a cotton sheet and rushed to Malcolm's side.

"His face is badly cut but he'll be all right," Avila said.

Kathleen saw Lundy release his grip on the embedded scalpel. His hand twitched once or twice and then stopped moving. He lay still, in a pool of his own blood.

He's gone! He's dead!

Her ordeal was finally over, her fears subsided, and Kathleen felt relief.

Avila helped Malcolm to his feet and said, "Keep this bandage pressed to your face until you get medical treatment."

Kathleen put her arm around Malcolm. "You're safe, you're going to be all right."

Fatso hugged Kathleen. "You did it! You saved Malcolm's life! You saved everybody's life!"

Fatso looked at Lundy's lifeless body and nudged it with his toe. "He's dead… I mean doornail dead… I've never seen so much blood."

Avila said, "We'd better get help." He looked at Fatso. "Mr Turner, go to the classroom and tell Professor Lupei to call the police. Ask him to come here and tend to Mr Paul and Miss Matthews."

Kathleen's clothes were soaked in blood. Her heart raced and breathing was difficult. She felt cold and began to shiver uncontrollably.

Avila said, "You're going into shock."

He said to Malcolm, "There's a blanket in the storage room."

Malcolm hesitated. Avila nodded towards Lundy's body and said, "It's all right, Mr Paul. He's dead."

Malcolm brought a thick wool blanket and placed it over Kathleen's shoulders. He whispered, "You were incredibly brave, Kathleen. I owe you my life."

He held her hand.

Chapter 58 Convocation

Three Years Later

Convocation seating was alphabetical which meant that Kathleen sat several rows back. Having attended the rehearsal and reception the evening before, she was fully prepared for the simple, but important, ceremony. Her friend and classmate, Claire Winters, also graduated. They were the first two women graduates in medicine from McGill.

There were approximately five hundred degrees to be awarded that morning and Kathleen waited patiently for her name to be called.

An hour later, the registrar called her name and added she was the gold medal winner in medicine. He praised her *Summa Cum Laude* achievement. His announcement received an enthusiastic round of applause. She walked across the stage and knelt before the Chancellor. He fitted her with a hood of scarlet cloth lined with dark blue silk. She saw her happy-looking parents in the audience, picked up her degree, and returned to her seat. She examined her degree and translated the Latin inscription, *Doctorem Medicinae et Chirurgiae Magistrum* as Doctor of Medicine and Surgery, Teacher. She was especially proud of the *Summa Cum Laude* inscription.

When the Convocation ceremony ended, Kathleen walked into bright sunshine. She looked for her parents. They stood beneath an oak tree and she ran towards them with open arms and a broad smile.

"Dr Matthews, give me a big hug," her father said, and wrapped her in his arms.

Her mother kissed her on the cheek and said, "I'm so very proud of you, Kathleen."

A dark, thickset man emerged from the crowd. He was dressed in a suit and it took a moment before Kathleen recognized Mike Avila.

He said, "Congratulations Kathleen, I'll never forget what you did."

"Thank you Mr Avila, for all you've done for me these past few years."

Vic Pratt stood on a grassy knoll, some distance away. She waved and he shaded his eyes from the sun and returned her greeting.

She felt a gentle touch on her shoulder and turned to see Mickey Clancy, looking nervous and wringing his cloth cap. "I just had to come and see you on your big day."

"Thanks Mickey, who knows, we just might work together again."

Mickey furrowed his brow. "Do you know something I don't know?"

Kathleen laughed. "Maybe, but I'm not telling."

Mickey smiled and walked away.

A loud insistent voice called her and, her best friend, Audrie Oakes, squeezed towards her.

Kathleen said, "Congratulations Audrie. I hear you'll be teaching English next semester."

Audrie replied, "Thank you, I'm excited. It's a probationary position at Montréal High but I'm hoping it will lead to better things."

Audrie said, "Dr Kathleen Matthews. You did it! You showed them all."

Audrie saw another friend and said, "I've got to go, I'll see you tonight at the Graduation Ball"

In the hurly-burly of the occasion, Kathleen lost sight of her parents and went looking for them. They were talking to a man with his back to her.

She approached and he turned to greet her. "Congratulations, Miss Matthews, or, should I say, Dr Matthews."

"Thank you Inspector Bouvette, what brings you here today?" she asked.

Her father interrupted, "It's Chief Bouvette. You might want to congratulate our newly appointed Chief of Police."

Kathleen said, "Congratulations Chief Bouvette. We'll all feel safer with you on the job."

"Thank you, Miss Matthews. To answer your earlier question, my youngest brother just graduated with a degree in law."

Kathleen replied, "Québec's justice system will be well served."

Bouvette said, "Thank you. I see my brother waving me over so I'll bid you *au revoir*. I hope to see you again, soon."

Her mother said, "People are leaving for the luncheon reception. Perhaps we should make our way over there. Do you have the tickets, Tom?"

"They're here in my pocket, "TJ said, patting his breast pocket.

They walked the short distance to the dining hall. Kathleen paused on the steps and looked behind at the long and colourful stream of gowned graduates, professors, university officials, happy relatives and friends.

She was about to enter the building when she felt a tug on her elbow. "Excuse me, Miss Matthews."

She recognized the voice. How could she forget?

"Well, if it isn't our intrepid reporter, Jimmy Moyer," she said.

"Got a minute?" he asked.

She replied, "Whenever I hear that, I think, trouble."

"Not today Miss Matthews, not today. Today is a good news day, certainly for you."

"How so?" Kathleen said with a wry smile.

"I asked my editor if I might cover the story of the first women graduates in medicine. Do you have a few minutes to answer some questions?"

"I thought you were a crime reporter, Mr Moyer. Since when does graduation in medicine constitute a crime?"

He laughed. "This is a special assignment, just for me. I thought, after all you've been through, people might be interested in your achievements as well as your challenges. It'll only take a minute. Besides, my three-year-old daughter may want a career in medicine one day."

Her mother said, "We'll go in and find our seats, you can catch up."

She answered Moyer's questions about her challenges and achievements. He thanked her for the interview and as he was leaving, Kathleen asked, "Did they ever catch the man who escaped with Lundy?"

He replied, "I'm afraid not. He seems to have disappeared off the face of the earth."

She said, "With Chief Bouvette on the job, I'm sure they'll catch him."

He replied, "If he does, I'll be there to report it."

A few minutes later, Kathleen checked the posted list at the entrance to the hall and found her table. The room was abuzz with conversation. Fifteen hundred people, seated at tables of eight, were in a mood to celebrate. Claire Winters and her parents were seated at her table.

Claire leaned across the table and said, "It was a struggle at times, Kathleen, but, we did it."

"I'm glad we did it together, I don't know if I could have done it without you."

Professor Merrick approached Kathleen and said, "Might I speak with you in private?"

Kathleen excused herself and followed Professor Merrick to an alcove, just off the kitchen.

"I've just received confirmation of my appointment as Director of the Montréal Neurological Institute. It's not official, so please keep it just between us, for now. I will approve your internship at the Institute as soon as I take office next week. I look forward to working with you."

Kathleen barely suppressed her joy. "Thank you Professor Merrick. I can't tell you how much I appreciate your support and encouragement."

Kathleen returned to the table and her father said, "You look happy Kathleen, did you get some good news?"

Kathleen's said, "Yes, it's the good news I've been waiting for."

Her parents exchanged knowing glances and Claire winked at her.

Following the luncheon, Kathleen and her parents were in the parking lot, standing next to her father's new, six-cylinder, Pierce-Arrow when she heard someone call her name.

Malcolm Paul hurried towards her and said, "Congratulations Dr Matthews. I wish you well in your future work, I know you'll be a success. Let's keep in touch."

"Thank you, Malcolm."

"My father's waiting, I'll see you tonight at the Graduation Ball."

"I'll save you a dance," she replied.

She saw Malcolm's father standing beside a sleek, black, limousine. Richard Paul waved to her and she waved back.

She squeezed between her father and mother and said, "Let's go home."

***

About the Author

Roland MacInnis lives in Kanata, Ontario, Canada. He started writing in 2011. His writing includes both fiction and nonfiction. He is married to Judy and has three children and six grandchildren.

Other Books by Roland MacInnis

Please visit your favorite e-book retailer to discover other books by Roland MacInnis.

Quarry [Book 1]
Bad Man Running [Book 2]
10 Tips for Leaders

Contact the Author

rolandnovel@gmail.com

www.ingramcontent.com/pod-product-compliance
Lightning Source LLC
Chambersburg PA
CBHW071258170626
46809CB00001B/270